Cannonball 204

Cannonball 204

A Lineage Series Novel

Michael Paul Hurd

Lineage Independent Publishing

Marriottsville, MD

ISBN (paperback): 9781958418284
First Printed in the United States

Publisher: Lineage Independent Publishing,
Marriottsville, MD

Maryland Sales and Use Tax Entity: Lineage Independent Publishing, Marriottsville, MD 21104

Contact: hurdmp@lineage-indypub.com

Website: https://lineage-indypub.com

Contents

1: History Lessons
September 5-6, 2017

My name is Marcus Aurelius Harris and I recently retired from the United States Navy, settling like many military retirees do in the Tidewater area of Virginia. Services for military retirees in that area are abundant and the cost of living will not entirely consume my military pension. At some point, I will have to find employment to make ends meet, but I am in no rush as I had amassed considerable savings, thanks to hazardous duty pay and being in locations where there were really no opportunities to spend my entire salary.

Most of my Navy career was spent as a diver. Only 44 years old at my retirement, I was eager to try recreational diving in one of the Great Lakes.

I chose Lake Erie because it offered challenging conditions, minimal depths, and warmer water than the deep (and cold) Lake Superior or the unpredictable Lake Michigan. The western end of Lake Erie, between the outflow of the Detroit River and Sandusky, Ohio, was also rich with naval history, having been the area of operations for Navy legend Oliver Hazard Perry in the War of 1812, and especially the "Battle of Lake Erie" that took place in September 1813.

Lake Erie was once the most polluted of the Great Lakes, having become the downstream cesspool and chemical dumping ground for industrial cities like Detroit, Toledo, and Cleveland. Thanks to President Nixon's Clean Water Act of 1972 and agreements signed between the United States and Canada, pollution of the lake had been significantly reduced, making it safer for recreational activities like swimming, diving, and fishing. The biggest challenge to diving in Lake Erie was reported to be underwater visibility, a situation in which I was quite comfortable. Very few of my Navy dives were in crystal-clear waters like Cozumel or Eilat. In fact, many were covert dives in the dark, supporting SEAL operations.

I arrived on the last ferry from Sandusky to South Bass Island on the day after Labor Day. From the ferry landing, I walked and checked into a tiny bed-and-breakfast for the next few days in the village of Put-in-Bay while I awaited the arrival of my old Navy buddy and mentor, retired Master Chief Sean Hagerty, on his boat, the *Maumee Marauder*.

The *Maumee Marauder* was a wide-beamed triple pontoon boat and set up for diving and salvage operations – ideally suited for the sort of dives I wanted to make. Hagerty, however, could no longer dive as he had suffered a severely ruptured eardrum in one of his last Navy dives. Instead, he hired salvage-qualified divers, like me, who had Navy experience. I had refused his earlier job offer as I did not wish to jeopardize our friendship.

On South Bass Island, my hosts, James Wilcox and his wife, Jacqueline (Jacqui, to her friends), were most gracious and invited me into their home for dinner, as the village's only eatery had closed about an hour before the ferry arrived. They had been lifelong residents of the island and had acquired the B&B when the so-called "housing bubble" burst in 2006.

The Wilcoxes were both experts on the history of the Lake Erie islands. They knew everything there was to know about the Battle of Lake Erie, including some of the folklore where abandoned equipment might have been lost to the depths. It was these legends that I wanted to explore.

Tongues loosened by copious amounts of alcohol, including some incredibly good homebrew made by James himself, we talked well into the early morning hours. During our discussions, James told me how Perry initially held the tactical advantage but lost it to the British because of light winds and reliance on new guns, called *carronades*.

Carronades were excellent weapons for delivering hull-destroying balls and anti-personnel shot, but only at close range. The British fleet, on the other hand, relied on longer-range cannon and battered Perry's approaching ships for over 20 minutes before they were in carronade range to return fire.

I was not concerned that 204 years had passed since that battle in 1813. My experience told me that storms, especially those over shallow water like Lake Erie, brought rough and erosive conditions both above and below the surface. It was this turbulence that would uncover previously buried artifacts, leaving them exposed for salvage and recovery. In fact, a so-called "100-year storm" had hit the area about two weeks before my arrival, increasing the likelihood of previously buried artifacts rising to the top of the silt on Lake Erie's bottom.

* * * * *

I retired from the Navy as a Senior Chief Petty Officer, rated as an Explosive Ordnance Disposal Master, with diving qualifications. I spent my entire 26-year Navy career in ocean and seaport diving, usually around things that could go "boom!" in the blink of an eye.

Underwater, explosives are even more dangerous than those on land. Submerged explosions create a severe overpressure situation that can immediately incapacitate anyone or anything near the blast, sometimes with fatal results. Sadly, I knew several sailors who met their end this way.

My Navy training had taken me to shallow-water wrecks around the world, some of which were remains from World War I or earlier. It always amazed me that, even after so many years, new artifacts would be uncovered by time and tide. Salvage, on the other hand, was always difficult and required specialized equipment to bring heavier items to the surface. I knew that Sean Hagerty would have the proper equipment.

*   *   *   *   *

The technical details of our upcoming dives were the original focus of our late-night discussions, but I was curious how both James and Jacqui had become experts on the history of the area.

"Marcus," James began, "I have a family tie to this region, and more importantly to Fort Malden up the Detroit River close to Lake Saint Clair."

"Do tell," I encouraged.

"You see, one of my ancestors, a Doctor Stephen Wilcox, was an Army surgeon who was taken prisoner in the Battles of Frenchtown, which at the time was in the Michigan Territory. Legend has it that he was one of only a handful of survivors of the River Raisin Massacre. Frontier documentation being somewhat incomplete, we believe that Stephen Wilcox eventually married and settled somewhere in the Michigan Territory west of Detroit after the war.”

“What massacre? Why had I never heard of it?” I asked.

“The War of 1812 was not as well-documented as some of our other wars, though it has been called ‘America’s Second War for Independence.’ For some reason, it has only been of interest to military historians. There were many significant battles that proved the United States could defend itself against hostile forces, but the Battles of Frenchtown were somewhat of an embarrassment, especially to General James Winchester.

“Winchester had superior numbers and actually won the first skirmish, but his forces were not well-trained nor well disciplined, consisting mostly of backwoods militiamen from Kentucky. Perhaps gloating from their initial victory that pushed the British and their confederated Native American allies out of Frenchtown, they were surprised four days later by a counterattack that killed nearly 400 Americans and resulted in about 550 being taken prisoner, including General Winchester.”

“So how does Doctor Wilcox fit into all of this?” I asked.

James continued, “Wilcox was left behind to care for a group of wounded men while the main body of the prisoners were force-marched north to Fort Malden. The wounded were allegedly left because they were unable to keep up the pace.

They fell behind and were set upon by bands of Potawatomi and Wyandot tribesmen loyal to the British. The figures have never been verified, but it is believed that as many as 100 men were killed. Stephen Wilcox, fortunately, was spared and allowed to rejoin the main body of captives heading for Fort Malden. He remained there until the fort was abandoned by British General Procter in the fall of 1813, about a month after the so-called Battle of Lake Erie.

"Even as a captive, Stephen kept impeccable records. Some of his notes and case files survived and are in the Michigan state archives."

"Wow. That is quite impressive, James," I replied. "So, I guess this Doctor Wilcox is real, unlike many genealogical legends in family trees?"

"As real as you and me," James answered, cocking his head and raising an eyebrow.

2: Diving Operations
September 7-9, 2017

The next morning, I received a cell phone call from Sean. He was on the lake, about an hour away from the main Put-in-Bay marina. I asked the Wilcoxes if they would save a breakfast for my friend as he would be checking into the B&B as soon as his boat was made fast in its slip. They were more than happy to do so.

My reunion with Hagerty was typical for former comrades-in-arms. It was as if our time apart had never existed. We spoke the same language, had shared similar experiences, and, like all military veterans, were awash with "war stories" of times and places over a decades-long career.

Over breakfast and copious amounts of hot coffee – always black and never sweetened, as was the tradition for Navy Chief Petty Officers, we planned our activities for the next few days. As Sean needed a spotter on the boat, he invited James Wilcox to join us.

Jacqui Wilcox accompanied us to the marina. She was quite observant, and I caught her staring at me several times as I donned my wetsuit. It seemed to be a lustful stare, like she had never seen a partially unclad male body before. I did my best not to acknowledge her, not even when she licked her lips seductively. *"What was she thinking?"* I wondered. She was a very attractive woman and a distraction I did not need. She was also married.

Sean and I slipped easily back into our operational tempo. We had worked together often enough that we rarely needed to speak. If we did speak, it was in a verbal shorthand that we both understood. I still had to stay focused on our work; loss of focus could prove fatal to a diver. When everything was ready, we pushed off from the pier. Jacqui waved to us but only James waved back. *"That should tell her something!"* I thought to myself, hoping that her flirtatious advances would be put to rest.

Sean's workboat was equipped with the latest electronics. It had radar, side-looking sonar, GPS, and AIS, all of which would be useful to map potential dive sites. James was amazed by the technology; he had never had more than passive exposure to modern marine electronics.

Lake Erie that afternoon was flat calm, so we took advantage of the conditions to mark out the boundaries of our dive area. Sean dropped marker buoys to establish a roughly square area of operations where the sonar had picked up what looked to be metallic objects on the lake bottom. The chart plotter recorded the depths in the area as between 15 and 35 feet, ideal for extended single-tank dives with no decompression stops.

After about three hours, we had enough information to plan the next day's dive. Weather permitting, we would motor to the northwest corner of the square, drop anchor, and raise the "Diver Below" flags. Once the safety protocols and gear checks were complete, I would be over the side and slowly exploring the bottom of Lake Erie.

We returned to the B&B about an hour before sunset, where Jacqui had already laid a cook-out in the picnic pavilion a few feet from the shore. She had prepared ribs, chicken, grilled vegetables, and roasted corn-on-the-cob, all to be washed down with more of James's wonderful homebrew. Punctuated by a spectacular sunset, it certainly was a night to remember.

We agreed that we should begin each day's dive around 11 a.m. and cease no later than 3 p.m. to take advantage of the better illumination from the sun still being more or less overhead during those hours. I would be equipped with an underwater camera affixed to the top of my mask to record the position of anything I discovered on the bottom that might be worthy of salvage. My mask would also be equipped with an underwater wireless communications unit so that I could have constant voice contact with Sean and James on the *Maumee*

Marauder. That would eliminate the need for a comms wire tether and allow me the freedom to both maneuver and remain submerged for longer periods.

We also towed James's small Rigid Inflatable Boat, or RIB, to the dive sites. If I needed to raise anything from the bottom with inflatable lifting bags, it would be easier and safer to recover them with a dinghy than to up anchor and recover them with the dive boat itself.

Minutes after reaching the bottom on the first dive, on September 7, I was astonished to see numerous half-exposed cannonballs in a depth of about 25 feet. The first one I picked up to examine was a small six-pounder, likely from a British cannon. Nearby, I could see several much larger (and heavier) carronade balls and heavier 12-pounders that probably had been fired from American ships, perhaps the *Niagara* or the *Lawrence*.

"Sean, do you copy? Over." I said into my microphone.

"Loud and clear, Marcus. Go."

"The bottom is literally covered with cannon and carronade balls. We may have found the mother lode. Over."

"Do you intend to raise any of them to the surface? Over."

"Yes, but the lifting bags can handle only one carronade or about half a dozen of the smaller cannonballs. Over."

"Roger. Let us know when you are ready to float the first bag. Over."

"Will do. Marcus out."

I set busily to work filling a net with six of the cannonballs and affixing four bright yellow lifting bags, which I inflated from an auxiliary cannister of compressed air affixed to my Buoyancy Control Device, or BCD. Once again, I radioed the boat.

"Sean, do you copy? Over."

"Loud and clear. Go."

"One lifting bag with six cannonballs to the surface in five… four… three… two… one." I inflated the final bag with the BCD and watched the net slowly ascend to the surface. "Acknowledge visual, please. Over."

"Yellow bags sighted about 30 yards east of my position. Dispatching dinghy. Over."

"Roger. Will remain below 15 feet so James can use the motor. Marcus out."

James used the electric outboard motor to take the dinghy to the lifting bag. He quickly secured the bag to the bow cleat and returned to the *Maumee Marauder*, where Sean assisted with getting the heavy shot on board.

With the next four bags, I raised one of the carronade balls to the surface. Again, James picked it up and took it to the *Marauder.* I checked the dive computer on my wrist and realized that I would have to return to the surface for a fresh tank of air in about twenty minutes. That allowed me enough time to explore the area a little more before heading up.

This would be our routine for the next several days, each time from a new anchorage. Dive. Inflate. Recover. Repeat.

3: Everyone Has A Story
September 7-9, 2017

With three men to share the burden of unloading our salvaged cannonballs and other artifacts, it didn't take us very long after docking to be ready to return to the B&B. That kind of exertion left us ravenous and Jacqui anticipated our hunger in the food she laid out. Each of the three nights were different, but plentiful, and there was always some of James's homebrew or very good wine from local wineries.

After-dinner conversation was always about our lives and experiences. Sean and I were at somewhat of a disadvantage, as we could not talk about some of the things we had seen or the places we had been. It did stifle the conversation at times, but we could talk about non-operational aspects of our lives. That usually meant talking about our past and our upbringing.

I told the story of how my parents were both killed in a car accident on I-75 just south of Monroe, Michigan, when I was eight years old. According to the instructions in my parents' wills, I was placed into the care of my maternal grandparents – both of whom were independently wealthy, "very busy people," they would always say, "and no time for children."

Their lack of concern for and disengagement from my welfare was unnerving for a boy my age. They also could not understand the teasing and bullying I had endured because of my middle name. "It's a perfectly wonderful name. It's classy and shows refinement," they would always say. I pleaded with them to let me go live with my other grandparents, but they were adamant that I had to remain with them as it was my mother's dying wish.

My own desires notwithstanding, it seemed they wanted to get rid of me and were not afraid to throw their money around to that end. So, when I entered Seventh Grade I was sent to a Catholic boarding school for boys; I remembered that it was near Detroit. "I can still see Sister Mary Grace and her ruler in our Latin classes. One wrong conjugation and it was 'whack!' across the back of the hand with her ruler," I recalled.

"Oh, you poor dear!" Jacqui exclaimed. "It must have been terrible." I had to look away from her baleful, doe-eyed expression.

"I managed, in spite of the 'old school' disciplinarian nuns," I explained. "Their corporal punishment, which Michigan outlawed at the end of my 10th Grade year, gave me a high tolerance for pain, something that translated well when I joined the Navy after graduating from high school two years later."

Sean gave a knowing smile; he knew full well what a high pain tolerance meant to someone undergoing Basic Underwater Demolition/SEAL, or BUD/S, training.

I continued, "In high school, I became what some of the guys called 'a jock's jock.' If it involved physical activity and endurance, I was part of it. Running with full football gear? No problem! Cross-country track in the spring? Bring it on! People were amazed that someone with my muscular build could compete – and win – in cross-country races. When I wasn't in practice for a particular sport, I was in the weight room or out on the track running. I guess it was my way of compensating for what my grandparents, the nuns, and the bullies had done to me."

Jacqui went next. Her story was less visceral than mine, but still told a story of neglect and indifference. She recounted how she lost her mother at the tender age of five. Her father never remarried.

"When I started getting curves," she said with a blush, "he didn't know how to handle me. I was left on my own to learn about being a woman. Like you, Marcus, I was the only child of only children, and both of my grandmothers were long gone as well. There was no one I could really turn to with my questions – and I had lots of them, especially after I discovered boys. I was so naïve…"

Sean Hagerty was next. "My life story is a lot less dramatic than either of yours. I had both of my parents all the way through high school and well into my adulthood. Because of my elite status within the Navy, they were always bragging about me, though I could tell them precious little about where I had been or what I had done. They relished the fact that they could tell their friends that I was 'away on some hush-hush assignment' or something like that."

"My life is probably the most boring of any of ours," James Wilcox moaned. "I went straight to college, lived in the dormitories, went to grad school and finally got my PhD. There are times when I wonder why I chose mathematics instead of history for my major."

I noticed that neither James nor Jacqui had mentioned anything at all about meeting each other. There seemed to be palpable tension between them. Maybe their B&B had come upon hard times. Maybe one (or both) of them was having an affair. That was something I found hard to believe as South Bass Island was not all that large and all of the year-round residents knew each other. They seemed to be totally focused on the business and had little spare time for outside friendships. Curious, I decided to press them for more information.

Turning to the Wilcoxes, I asked, "So how did the two of you meet?"

Jacqui was quick to reply. "I worked at the pizza parlor near the college where James was doing his undergrad work. His sparkling smile, twinkling eyes, and impish demeanor captivated me from the moment I laid eyes on him." With her statement, something seemed to change between them; it was like the tension in the air had suddenly dissipated.

"So, it was love at first sight?" Sean asked, rejoining the conversation.

"Not entirely," James replied. "It took me some time to come around to the idea that this gorgeous young woman had the hots for me – "

"James!" she interrupted, playfully slapping his upper arm. "Couldn't you have put that a little more diplomatically?" *"Well, I certainly did have the hots for him once upon a time,"* she thought to herself.

Jacqui continued, "Unfortunately, we couldn't have children, so we doted on James's nieces and nephews. What he didn't tell you is that he is from a very large family: four sisters and five brothers. They are scattered out all over the United States and they rarely visit us here in this little tourist trap of a town."

It sounded to me that Jacqui was at times unhappy with their decision to acquire the B&B and live on South Bass Island. Her mood had changed from playful to grumpy in the blink of an eye.

4: At the Memorial
September 10, 2017

Sunday, September 10, 2017, was a beautiful day. Daylight spread from the eastern horizon to an almost cloudless sky and the winds were light and variable. It was much like the conditions Oliver Hazard Perry experienced as he prepared his Lake Erie fleet to do battle against the British. The island was preparing for a commemoration of the so-called "Battle of Lake Erie," that was to begin at 11:45 a.m., the recorded time of the first shot in the battle.

Re-enactors dressed in 1813 military uniforms had been arriving on South Bass Island since noon on September 9. They assembled in the park surrounding the Victory and International Peace Memorial, which was a growing tent city as each wave of re-enactors arrived. As Marcus, James and I had all been involved in the recovery of significant artifacts during the past week, we were madly working to put those on display for the expected throngs of visitors.

It was backbreaking work, moving and stacking the recovered cannon and carronade balls at the designated location in the park. James's utility vehicle and its dump bed were ideally suited to the task, as it was configured for hauling construction materials and landscaping equipment. I was responsible for stacking the cannonballs, all 204 of the six-pounders that we had recovered in my dives during the past week. I tried not to think that I would be moving half a ton of cast iron in the process.

As I stacked, I noticed that each of them had a foundry marking, usually a symbol of some kind rather than alphanumeric designators. The markings were done to enable later identification of the rounds as the artillery unit or naval ship tracked its non-exploding ordnance for later identification and possible re-use in a future battle.

In a previous life, James Wilcox had taught mathematics at the Metropolitan Campus of Cuyahoga Community College, affectionately known as 'Tri-C', in Cleveland. He told me that if I stacked the cannonballs in a pyramid with an 8x8 base, the peak would be the 204th ball. I chuckled at the thought of trying to stack 204 round objects. It reminded me of "field days" during the early days of my Navy career – one of those useless and mundane tasks performed by unrated and low-ranking enlisted sailors on casual shore duty while awaiting assignment to a ship or an "A School."

Starting just before sun-up, I patiently worked through the stack, taking time to rest my back every few minutes while

James returned to the B&B to load more cannonballs. When he returned, we would work together to unload them as close as possible to my growing pyramid. All in all, it took us roughly two hours to move and stack them.

200… 201… 202… 203… one left to place on the peak of the pyramid. Up to this point, they had all been marked with a simple diamond with a circle circumscribed around it. The last ball had a very strange marking. It was more of a circle with a series of smaller and more ornate circles inside it, looking almost like a maze from an English estate's garden. There was something familiar about the concentric circles, but I could not remember why.

As I picked up the last cannonball, I felt a strange vibration. It appeared to be emanating both from the ground under my feet and from number 204 itself. The vibration increased as I approached the nearly completed stack. It reminded me of subtle changes in engine pitch aboard Navy ships. *"Why is this memory surfacing now?"* I wondered almost aloud.

Shaking off the vibrations as just a manifestation of my Navy past, I reached out to place the final ball on the pyramid. It felt so much heavier than all the rest, yet at the same time lighter. It seem to be attracted to the four balls on the layer below, as if a magnet was pulling the stack together. That wasn't possible, though. The cannonballs were made of lead and non-magnetic!

Cannonball 204 clicked solidly in place and an eerie aura of blue light seemed to emanate from within the pyramid. That light was accompanied by a very disturbing high-pitched sound. It was so disturbing that I may have blacked out for a few seconds.

Shaking my head to clear the remnants of the sound from my aural nerves, I looked around and saw that I was surrounded by men in 1813 uniforms of the United States Navy. The officers were resplendent in their cocked hats, shoulder boards and starched collars; the enlisted men were obvious, dressed in their red-striped working shirts and white trousers. Women, too, were dressed in period costume of long dresses, petticoats, and wimples. *The commemoration seems to have already started,"* I thought. *"But it's only just after 7 a.m."* I was confused.

"You, there! Stand fast!" an officer bellowed. I ignored him as best I could.

He bellowed again, "I said 'stand fast!'"

Startled, I stopped in my tracks and stood reflexively to attention. Was this strutting martinet talking to me? It seemed he might be taking his role a little *too* seriously, reminding me of "90-day blunder" Ensigns without a lick of naval knowlege.

I couldn't be sure as I had not been assigned a role in the re-enactment, other than to dress as an Ordinary Seaman, in white trousers and blue jacket appropriate for shore duty and be prepared to explain the significance of our recovered artifacts.

"Sir?" I questioned, quickly getting into character.

"Load those shot into a limber and take them to the pier for loading onto the *Niagara* and be quick about it. She sets sail as soon as Master Commandant Perry gives the word."

"Aye, sir," I replied. I had just finished building the stack and here this ass was asking, no, ordering me to dismantle it.

I took stock of my surroundings once more. The monument was gone. The B&B's location was open space. The shoreline was abuzz with naval activity and there were masted sailing vessels tied up to the pier. Was it some sort of trick? Perhaps James's homebrew was a little more potent than we thought. Then there was this 'Master Commandant Perry' guy. All of the naval history books gave his title as 'Commodore.' Could it be that I was no longer in 2017? I felt the blood draining from my face as I blanched, trying not to vomit.

"Sir, permission to speak?" I asked weakly.

"Granted."

"What year is this?"

"What year? Are you an idiot? Why, it's the Year of Our Lord Eighteen Hundred and Thirteen! Sailor, have you slept through the past nine months or were you just drunk off your feet?" I tried not to look too astonished by his response and resisted an even stronger urge to lose the contents of my stomach.

Mysteriously, I had been transported across time to 1813. Was I dreaming? It looked as though I was about to experience the Battle of Lake Erie first-hand. It was no coincidence that I had been stacking cannonballs on the morning of the anniversary of the battle, 204 years later. The significance of that last cannonball was now crystal clear.

Following orders was second nature to me. As a Senior Chief Petty Officer, a rank that didn't exist until 1958, I had been conditioned to sometimes question and challenge the orders of the officers appointed over me. The present situation was *not* one of those. I consciously decided that obeying the officer's orders (in spite of my initial impression of him) was in my best interest. My studies of naval history told me that I could be thrown in the brig and subsequently flogged for insubordination. That was a punishment I had no desire to endure.

I was fatigued from stacking the cannonballs before… whatever it was that had just happened to me… but somehow found the strength to load them into the limber cart. I once again went through the mental calculation of the effort necessary to move over a ton of lead – again. "I'll sleep well tonight!" I whispered to myself.

Back and forth I went, moving about a dozen of the cannonballs in each load. The task took me close to two hours to complete. Knowing the timetable of the battle as I did, Perry's Lake Erie Fleet and his flagship, the *Lawrence*, should be sailing out of Put-in-Bay within the hour. I somehow felt compelled to be aboard either the *Lawrence* or the *Niagara*.

5: Into Thin Air
September 10, 2017

James and Sean were returning to the cannonball display from their rented salvage shed next to the Put-in-Bay Marina. The only things left for them to move were the much heavier carronade balls. They weighed around 32 pounds each.

Driving across the green to the pyramid Marcus had assembled, James noticed that Marcus was nowhere to be seen. "He must have had to go take a leak or something. All that coffee he drank earlier must have gone right through him!" James teased. He saw a row of about a dozen portable toilets about 100 yards away, screened from the green by a mural painted on a canvas screen. Only the roofs of the toilets were visible. It was possible that Marcus could be in one of them.

"Let's just wait a few minutes before we dump this load in case Marcus needs it somewhere else," Sean replied. "The dump bed makes unloading easy, but having to reload all of this will be back-breaking work."

James cut the engine. Being an off-road vehicle, the tractor was not required to have any noise suppression and was very noisy. Noise notwithstanding, it was a two-stroke and the smell of its exhaust was intense. "Better not get our visitors all riled up," James said with a wink and a nod. "There's not enough wind to clear the exhaust cloud before the visitors will start complaining."

Half an hour later, and there was still no sign of Marcus. There were now over 100 re-enactors milling about on the green, all dressed in period-appropriate naval uniforms. Marcus could have blended into the crowd, but he *did* have a job to do as a docent at the armaments display.

"Where could he have gone for this long?" Sean asked. "And why is that top cannonball on the ground beside the stack? Marcus would never have left something like that unfinished."

Sean picked up the errant cannonball from the grass and placed it at the top of the pyramid. Unlike Marcus's experience a little while earlier, Sean did not sense a magnetism emanating from within the stack, nor did he feel any vibrations under foot. He placed the final cannonball at the apex of the pyramid.

"There. It's now a complete stack," Sean commented, his tone deadpan. There was no vibration under foot, no unusual sounds, and no apparent gravitational attraction between the cannonballs. It was just a stack of artifacts from an almost-forgotten war.

"I don't know what could have happened to Marcus," James noted. "Let's drive over to the B&B and see if he might be there."

They pulled into the B&B's parking area. Like a flash, James was up the steps and into the kitchen. "Jacqui, have you seen Marcus?"

"The last time I saw him, he was taking the last cold gulp of his third… no… fourth cup of coffee and running out the door. He sure looked fine in his re-enactor uniform…" Her voice trailed off as she grasped a memory of James in his younger years, fit and trim. Regardless, Marcus was, in her mind's eye a much better specimen.

Sean broke through Jacqui's distraction. "We can't find him anywhere and the visitors will be arriving on the next ferry from Sandusky." Sean said, the agitation in his voice obvious to the Wilcoxes. Sean's combat training from the Navy and Marine Corps had inculcated a mantra of "improvise, adapt, and overcome." However, since his forced retirement a few years earlier, he had become less and less tolerant of ambiguity. Deviations from plans and schedules brought out the worst of his character.

"We have another half an hour until all 21st Century things need to be off the green," James reminded them in an effort to calm Sean's obvious agitation. "Let's go back to the cannonball stack and wait until the last possible minute."

Sean added his own sarcastic observation, "Marcus is sure to show up. It's not like him to miss an opportunity to show off." Sean knew his friend well.

Ten minutes ticked by, then twenty. At twenty-five minutes, James and Sean unconsciously started taking turns looking at their watches at thirty-second intervals. When the full half hour had passed, they looked at each other. Sean raised an inquisitive eyebrow, while James cocked his head to one side. Something was amiss and they both knew it.

6: Battle
September 10, 1813

I made it aboard the USS *Lawrence* and signed the ship's roster as an Able Seaman just as Perry was giving the order to cast off all lines and make sail. He was clearly ready for battle, wearing what we in the 20th Century would have called a 'game face.' Under his command were the USS *Lawrence* (his flagship), the USS *Niagara,* and seven other smaller vessels, the *Ariel,* the *Caledonia,* the *Scorpion,* the *Somers,* the *Porcupine,* the *Tigress,* and the *Trippe.*

I did my best to be inconspicuous. The noise and clamor of imminent battle overrode any hope of anonymity.

"Mister Harris, welcome aboard! Are you helm qualified?" Perry bellowed. He clearly had taken notice of my arrival.

"Aye, sir!" I responded sharply. *"Oh, my,"* I thought, *"I am serving under a United States Navy legend. If... when I get back to 2017, will anybody believe me that I was here?"*

"Set course north-by-northwest and tack as necessary."

"Course north by northwest, tacking as necessary. Aye."

The training I had received during a CPO Heritage Week aboard the *USS Constitution* shortly after donning Chief's khakis for the first time nearly a decade earlier… well… a 21st Century decade earlier, that is, served me in good stead. I "knew my ropes," thanks to that training.

We were underway and heading straight into the British squadron. Rounding Oak Point, Perry barked, "Mister Harris, adjust base course to west-by-southwest."

"Base course west by southwest. Aye."

It was about 11:00 a.m., or "six bells" in nautical parlance. In less than an hour, we would be in the maw of the British squadron led by the HMS *Detroit* under the command of Captain Robert Heriot Barclay. I hoped that I would not be among the two dozen or so killed in action during the battle. I tried not to dwell on the possibility of my permanent absence from the 20th Century if my timeline ended today.

Because we were departing from a sheltered cove on the leeward side of an island, we were at a significant disadvantage. Barclay's squadron had the weather gauge, or downwind advantage, as they were crossing open water from the east – forcing us to tack as Perry had ordered. It was slow going at first, with the light wind, and it seemed as though we waited an eternity for the first salvo from the *HMS Detroit*. The remainder of the United States flotilla was strung out in line formation behind us, with the *Niagara* immediately astern.

As I peered off into the distance trying to ascertain the *Detroit*'s intentions, Perry stood next to me. I was standing next to a legend of the United States Navy.

"Mister Harris, do you know that the *Lawrence* and the *Niagara* have the firepower to blast the *Detroit* out of the water? Our new guns, called 'carronades,' fire heavier rounds with more force than their long-range cannon."

I was being lectured by Oliver Hazard Perry!

Boom! A few seconds later, the whoosh of a cannon ball passing overhead was heard.

The first shot had been fired from the *Detroit*. It was roughly 11:45 a.m. Fortunately, it missed, splashing into the lake less than 100 yards in front of our bow. We had to close the range or risk being holed at the water line and sunk.

I looked up to the topmast and saw the wind pennant change direction almost imperceptibly. The winds were shifting! We could begin closing to counterattack.

"Mister Harris, make a course directly for the *Detroit*. Bring us into firing range," Perry ordered.

"Aye, sir."

"Gunners, make ready!" Perry bellowed.

"Gunners to the ready. Aye," the gunnery officer replied in confirmation.

Gradually, the distance to the British flotilla began to close.

Belowdecks was a flurry of activity. The gunnery officer had his crews frantically (and mistakenly) loading their carronades with anti-personnel shot instead of their nominal 32-pound projectiles that would do considerably more damage to the target ship's timbers. The two 12-pounder long-range cannon – for which I had hauled most of the ammunition -- were readied as well, but their position in the bow of the *Lawrence* put only one of them in a usable position at a time.

Before we closed the range to the *Detroit* and the *Queen Charlotte*, long guns from the two ships found their range to the *Lawrence.* I marveled at the accuracy of their fire from fixed guns without assistance from computers. The *Lawrence* was taking hit after hit and was quickly reduced to a floating wreck.

The smell of gunpowder, smoldering timbers, vomit, gore and human excrement were overshadowed by the moans and screams of the wounded and dying. There were too many wounded for the assistant surgeon to take care of; he was overwhelmed as the ship's surgeon had taken ill just before the battle commenced. I would later learn that 80 percent of the *Lawrence*'s crew was either wounded or killed. I was one of the fortunate ones, having only sustained a minor wound in my left forearm from flying debris.

With his flagship incapacitated and its last gun out of action, Perry ordered that he and his flag be transferred to the *Niagara*, about a half mile astern. I was one of the six men grabbed from the survivors to row Perry through heavy gunfire to his new flagship. How we managed to pass through the barrage of naval artillery and small arms fire without being hit is a mystery and probably a miracle. As we rowed, the *Lawrence* was surrendered to the British.

By a stroke of sheer luck, the *Detroit* collided with the *Queen Charlotte*, rendering both ships unfit for battle. The confusion was compounded by nearly every officer on both of the British ships being either severely wounded or killed, leaving a very junior lieutenant in command. At this point, I observed that there were only one or two British ships capable of continuing the battle.

Despite the confusion among the British and most of their fleet being disabled, they expected the *Niagara* to lead an American withdrawal from the fight. They were quite wrong. Instead, Perry rallied his flotilla and gained enough of a tactical advantage to fire broadside against the *Detroit* and *Queen Charlotte*, crippling their ability to respond. Both British ships surrendered at approximately 3 p.m. In his dispatch to General William Henry Harrison after the battle, Perry reported, "We have met the enemy and they are ours."

In the aftermath of the battle, Perry's flotilla would ferry over 2,500 American troops to Amherstburg, in Canada near the mouth of the Detroit River. I was part of the crew that delivered the first wave of these soldiers who would eventually capture Fort Amherstburg (colloquially known as Fort Malden) from the British.

Capture, I would later learn, was a significant overstatement as British General Procter had abandoned the fort and set fire to its buildings, burning most of the fort to the ground. The fort's armory, including its few cannons, had already been emptied to supply the British Lake Erie flotilla, leaving Fort Malden defenseless.

In a humane gesture, Procter had released all of the American prisoners held at Fort Malden, some since the beginning of the war. They were left with nothing more than the clothes on their backs and threadbare tents for shelter. Food was scarce and the departing British could not leave any behind, forcing the now-released prisoners to fish and forage for themselves. It was in the American tent city that I would meet a Doctor Wilcox, surgeon to the American prisoners of war. He had been taken prisoner after the Battle of the River Raisin earlier in 1813.

Could this be Doctor Stephen Wilcox, the ancestor of James Wilcox, the man who ran the B&B adjacent to the memorial park in 2017? I had to find out.

The memory of our alcohol-fueled discussions the night before Sean arrived was somewhat hazy. James did mention that there was a long line of medical men in his family, some of whom had become quite famous. It took some time, but I did finally remember James' mention of a Doctor Stephen Wilcox and the River Raisin Massacre.

7: The Two Doctors
September 1813, After the Battle of Lake Erie

As the American tent camp expanded around what was left of Fort Malden, I got to know more about Doctor Stephen Wilcox and a second surgeon left behind by the British. It was not unusual for us to spend our time together seated around a small campfire after the evening mean had been served to the officers and medical staff.

The British surgeon, Doctor Simon Smithwick, had resigned his position when British General Procter abandoned Fort Malden. Smithwick, I would learn, was not a career military surgeon. He was a volunteer doctor who had been sent to North America against his will along with reinforcements for the 41st Regiment of Foot.

Wilcox, who I was now pretty certain *was* James Wilcox's ancestor, claimed to be originally from the Hudson River Valley in New York. He said his grandparents settled in that region after the Seven Years' War as it was then known. He also bragged that he "had been trained in the finest teaching hospitals in New York City." Unmarried and living a bachelor life on the frontier at the eastern end of Lake Ontario near Oswego, New York, when the war broke out, he signed on with a militia regiment as its surgeon.

"Doctor Wilcox, why did you join the Army?" I asked one evening over a glass of something close to (but not quite) beer. The question was one of many I wanted answered.

Scratching his chin pensively, Wilcox replied, "I was not cut out to live on the frontier. I had no wife, no children, and no ties to the area, so signing on to a militia regiment seemed like a logical thing to do,"

"And you ended up a Prisoner of War… that must have been difficult," I commented.

Wilcox paused before answering. "I had to take care of the men. There was no other choice than to see to their needs. It was most unfortunate that we were caught up in the River Raisin situation. Never in my years as a physician and surgeon had I seen such atrocities inflicted on the human body. It was absolutely terrible." He looked off into the distance, trying to control his emotions, then continued, "There were bodies and parts of bodies everywhere. Some of the men's faces were so battered that I could not have recognized one man from the next. Some men were scalped; others had their private parts mutilated. It was most horrendous. There was nothing I could do for many of them, except sit and watch them die, if they were alive at all."

Wilcox's voice tailed off into silence as he buried his face in his hands and began sobbing uncontrollably. I surmised that this was the first time since the massacre some ten months earlier that he had been given an opportunity to unburden himself. I knew from the "wounded warrior" training I had received in my own time that talking about a horrific event was much better than keeping it all bottled up inside. Some wounds were mental with no evidence of physical injury.

While Wilcox was a POW at Fort Malden, he and Smithwick had become fast friends. They had much in common, including their outlook on standards of care, hygiene, and sanitation. They trusted each other's professional judgment implicitly.

We all stared pensively into the campfire for a few minutes before Doctor Smithwick spoke. For the moment, Wilcox remained silent as he worked to regain his composure.

"London was my home, but I studied medicine at the University of Edinburgh, in Scotland. I could have studied at any of the universities nearer to London but wanted to get away, to sow my wild oats, so to speak. My father, a man of the world, suggested that Edinburgh would be the ideal place for me to do that. From my own perspective, the fact that the University of Edinburgh is the preeminent medical school in the United Kingdom had nothing to do with it."

I was curious about how Smithwick ended up being an Army surgeon. "Did you volunteer for the Army?" I asked.

"In a manner of speaking, yes. I was spending some leisure time on the banks of the Firth of Forth after finally completing my studies. As all young men do, I was contemplating my next steps. On a whim, I visited an Army recruiting tent near Dreghorn Castle and decided on the spot to enter into His Majesty's service. Two years later, and here I am," Smithwick explained.

Finally having regained his composure, Doctor Wilcox rejoined the conversation. "Doctor Smithwick… Stanley… and I first worked together on an American militiaman who had originally escaped the River Raisin battles. I believe he was from Kentucky. Somehow, the poor lad had survived for over a week in the woods before he was captured by British soldiers and brought to Fort Malden.

"He was in a sorry state, badly infected, and already near death. We treated his wounds as best we could, but ultimately decided the case was hopeless. We told the soldier that his remaining time on earth would be short and that we would do everything in our power to make him comfortable. We also summoned a minister to offer prayer and spiritual comfort.

"In our discussions, I discovered that the soldier could neither read nor write. So… I allowed him to dictate a letter for me to send to his family in Albany. He died the next morning and is buried just over there in the graveyard." Wilcox pointed generally over his left shoulder before continuing, "Since then, Doctor Smithwick and I have worked on almost every case together. It didn't matter to us if the wounded man was allied with the British or was an American fighter. They all got the same standard of treatment. We are doctors first; our nationalities have had no impact on how we care for our patients."

I was in awe of these two men and how they were able to provide care and comfort in such horrendous conditions. They had no anesthesia, no antiseptics other than alcohol, and only minimal surgical equipment; nothing more than a few sharp knives, bone saws, rudimentary hemostats, and retractors. Yet, according to Doctor Wilcox's own case notes, the survival rate for wounded combatants was surprisingly high. In contrast, his records indicated that more than three-quarters of all deaths during his time at Fort Malden were from diseases.

As our campfire died down, the sounds of snoring, farting, and other things men do in the night began to overtake and drown out our conversation. I had to return to my quarters on the *Lawrence,* while the two doctors could simply retire to their shared tent adjacent to the campfire. I thought they had the better arrangement, as the conditions on board the *Lawrence* were far from ideal – and a far cry from the Chief Petty Officer quarters I had enjoyed during my time in the United States Navy of the 20th and 21st Centuries.

8: A Clue
Late September, 2017

Marcus Harris had been missing for a little more than two weeks. In that time, Sean Hagerty had taken the *Maumee Marauder* back to Toledo. He left his contact information behind with James and Jacqui Wilcox in case they turned up any leads on Marcus's whereabouts – or worse, his demise.

The Wilcoxes had only known Marcus for a matter of days but had quickly become friends. Jacqui in particular was quite smitten with the young Navy retiree. His muscular physique brought back pleasant memories of her husband, James, in his earlier days. She had realized long ago that the life of an academic involved a largely sedentary lifestyle, and no amount of yardwork or upkeep on the B&B was ever going to help James recover his youthful vigor. Jacqui sometimes laughed to herself that James's special blue pills generally only gave him a headache without producing the desired effect. Oh, how she missed those days (and nights, too)!

James had taken a much more didactic approach to examining what might have happened to Marcus. He knew that Marcus had no romantic affiliation with anyone of either gender; that eliminated the possibility of Marcus secreting himself away for a romantic tryst.

Could he have been the victim of foul play? Again, James deduced that there was no evidence of such an unlikely scenario. There were absolutely no clues to support that hypothesis; both the local police and Ottawa County Sheriff's Office had totally dismissed any wrongdoing that had resulted in Marcus Harris's disappearance.

James's study had been taken over by his analysis of Marcus's evanescence. It looked more like a police detectives' squad room than the office of a professor. James had outstanding Internet research skills and had done a deep dive on Marcus Harris, going back as far as his high school days in southeastern Michigan. Nothing conclusive. The most James was able to turn up was a newspaper clipping about Marcus's enlistment in the United States Navy in 1995. After that, Marcus Harris was simply a ghost and chasing that ghost was absorbing James Wilcox.

After several hours spent pondering the clues (or lack thereof), James heard the familiar sounds of floorboards squeaking. He knew it had to be Jacqui as their B&B was completely vacant except for the two of them. It was well after Labor Day and the tourist trade in northwestern Ohio had dried up. Most of the visitors now were day travelers or fishermen passing through the marina for fuel and supplies. Very few chose to spend the night docked in the marina's transient slips.

"Jacqui, there has to be something I am missing," James mused, his back still turned away from the door as he hunched over his keyboard.

Jacqui stood in the doorway wearing a diaphanous and nearly transparent negligee, with a peignoir draped loosely over her shoulders. "James, there really is *something* you are missing," she said in a sultry voice that meant business.

James almost didn't recognize his wife's voice. He turned to face the doorway. His eyebrows arched as he surveyed his wife's attire. He was speechless.

With her eyes locked on his, she let the peignoir fall to the floor, then walked slowly across the room to James's desk. Reaching him, she gently caressed his cheek with her fingertips. As her hand moved further down his chest, James suddenly reached out and grabbed her. The movement was almost as if he intended to slap her hand away.

"Can't you see I am busy?" he growled. "I have to solve what happened to Marcus!"

That was the straw that broke the camel's back. Jacqui turned on her heel, stomped to the door, picked up her peignoir and tromped loudly down the hall to their bedroom. Just before slamming the door, she screamed, "You can sleep in your study tonight, you… you… you inattentive and insufferable bastard!"

The next morning, Jacqui was still in high dudgeon over James's rejection the night before. Before heading to the kitchen for morning coffee, she made it a point to be as unappealing as possible: a threadbare flannel nightie, large curlers in her hair, her ugliest slippers on her feet, and, as a final touch, she had intentionally not yet brushed her teeth.

Jacqui poured herself a cup of coffee, resisting the urge to dump the scalding contents of the pot into James's lap. *"How would that be for something warm between your legs?"* she thought to herself with a wry smile. Moving to the dinette table with coffee in hand, she sat down with a plop. More than a little perturbed by her huffiness, James lowered his newspaper and glared at her. No words were spoken.

The verbal silence continued for quite some time. The only sounds were both of them annoyingly slurping their coffee while Jacqui fluffed through a magazine and Janes ceremoniously popped his newspaper with each turn of a page. It seemed that neither of them was going to give an inch. They'd had more than their share of squabbles like this in the past few months, with each more acrimonious than the one before.

Around 9 a.m., the silence was broken by the chiming of the front doorbell. As James was the more presentably dressed of the two, he answered the door.

"Mister Wilcox?" the college aged young man asked.

"Yes, I am James Wilcox," he replied.

"My name is Harold McGee. My friends call me Hal. I was in one of your freshman math classes at Tri-C, and I remember you saying that you were an amateur historian in addition to being a mathematics professor."

"Your memory serves you well, young man," James responded.

"Well, sir, I was walking near the pier this morning and found something in the mud that might be of interest." Hal explained. "I was working at the marina when you and that diver went out on the *Maumee Marauder* and recovered all of those cannonballs."

"That's correct," James said with a nod.

Hal reached into his pocket and pulled out a ball chain lanyard with two shiny objects attached. They made a very unmistakable sound when they clanked together: military dog tags.

"These belonged to a Marcus Aurelius Harris, blood type B-Positive, religious preference Lutheran. And of course, it also has his Social Security number," Hal said, trying not to laugh at the middle name.

"Marcus? He stayed here when we were doing the dives," James replied. "Most soldiers and sailors keep their dog tags as a memento of their military service. Some, especially the ones who retired, wear them for the rest of their lives. Marcus Harris was probably one of those men."

"Jacqui!" James called out loudly, "please come here."

She had already moved to the front parlor from the kitchen and had heard every word. As if by magic, she appeared at James's side, still in her frumpy accoutrements, but with the addition of a filthy, pilled and once pink terrycloth robe. The mere mention of Marcus's name made her shiver with excitement, no matter how she was dressed.

"Yes, James?" she answered.

"We have to let the police department know that this young man has recovered Marcus's dog tags. He would not have just left them behind." James paused, knowing the effect what he was about to say would have on Jacqui. "I think he might have drowned."

"It's a big leap to go from nothing to suggesting he drowned," Jacqui argued. "You don't have proof, and he was in perfect health." *"Too perfect,"* she mused to herself as her thoughts strayed. "If you think we should call the police, what are you waiting for?"

The Put-in-Bay police department was woefully undermanned and called in the Ottawa County Sheriff's Office to help with the investigation. After reviewing James's notes and examining the dog tags, they decided to call Sean Hagerty and the *Maumee Marauder* back from Toledo.

The Ottawa County Sheriff's Office had its own Marine Division and Underwater Rescue Team and probably could have handled the situation on their own. However, Hagerty had kept impeccable chart plotter records of the underwater terrain and the dives taken to recover the cannonballs, so it was a logical step to bring him back to assist with what was likely to be a recovery operation: Marcus, at this point, was "missing and presumed dead."

The Sheriff's divers all maintained their own equipment and were all rescue certified; however, they did not have the salvage experience nor the capacity to support extended dives like Sean Hagerty had aboard the *Marauder*. He made sure that they would all be equipped with state-of-the-art underwater comms gear, which was important for both safety and coordination of their search.

Conditions on Lake Erie were favorable and Hagerty reached Put-in-Bay about six hours after he was called. There was not quite enough daylight remaining for diving operations that day. There was really no rush, as the best they could hope for would be to find Marcus Harris's body entangled in underwater debris.

9: Orders
Late September, 1813

From Fort Malden, I learned that a sizeable force of cavalry under Kentucky militia Colonel Richard Mentor Johnson had taken Detroit without military action. Fort Malden was already in American hands and the combination gave the United States control of Lake Erie, cut off British supply lines, and expanded the advantage over the now-retreating forces under General Procter and Iroquois Confederacy leader Tecumseh.

I had asked to be transferred to the medical camp run by Doctors Wilcox and Smithwick in hopes of avoiding further conflict; however, my request was denied by Oliver Hazard Perry himself.

"Mister Harris, the United States Navy needs competent sailors like yourself. You performed admirably in our last battle and by the power vested in me by the President of the United States, James Madison, and Major General William Henry Harrison, I am breveting you as a Lieutenant in the United States Navy. You will be assigned to the USS *Lawrence* as its Executive Officer. Your duties will also include oversight of the captured British ships, the *Detroit* and *Queen Charlotte*."

"Aye, sir!" I responded enthusiastically with a sharp salute as Perry handed me a wax-sealed envelope with my written orders. Short of shore duty, it was the best possible outcome that would keep me away from battle. The *Lawrence*, along with the two captured British ships, had just been converted to floating hospitals, ready to receive the wounded from an imminent battle between American and British forces. Perry's written orders also placed Doctors Wilcox and Smithwick under my command and attached them to the hospital ships in addition to the makeshift camp adjacent to the remains of Fort Malden.

I still wasn't entirely comfortable in my new situation, jumping back in time 204 years. The time-honored (maybe 'time-worn' was more accurate?) traditions of the Navy made up for some of that uncertainty, but would I ever be able to get back to my own time? The only person that was likely to miss me was my cohort and mentor, Sean Hagerty.

I had made a conscious decision early in my Navy career not to become romantically entangled. The nature of my duties meant that someone likely would experience heartbreak, whether it be through incapacitating injury or a fatal event. My conscience would not let me foist that agony on anyone. I was an only child of two only children – so there was no other family outside of the Navy that would grieve my passing should anything untoward happen to me in a hostile situation.

I was brought out of my melancholy by the screams of a soldier enduring the agony of an amputation under the knife of Doctor Wilcox, who was now the senior surgeon for the *Lawrence* and Fort Malden. Ether was still over thirty years in the future and the best a wounded man could hope for was to be incoherently drunk when such procedures were performed. The poor soldier finally passed out from the pain; his screams were gut-wrenching.

I did learn that the good Doctor Wilcox was a pioneer and ahead of his time in antiseptic procedures. He insisted on clean surgical instruments, sterilized in alcohol whenever possible, and washed his hands so frequently that they looked like those of the camp-following washer women.

"Mister Harris, would you be so kind as to attend to this poor soul when he awakens?" Wilcox asked me as he scrubbed the blood from his hands following the amputation. I noticed that the soldier's hands were also bandaged, making his arms look like white clubs extending out from his shoulders. He would not be able to use his hands.

"Yes, Doctor," I replied. "Should I provide him with food and drink?"

"For now, he is to drink water only. We need to keep his kidneys working. If he can tolerate water and keep it down for six hours, you can provide him with weak honey water. The natural sugar will give him a little energy and also help prevent infection."

Wilcox continued, "When I return to examine him this evening, I will administer laudanum if he is in considerable pain," Wilcox explained. "Please take note that his hands are bandaged, not so much because of their wounds, but because I want to prevent him from disturbing the site of amputation when he regains consciousness."

With no small degree of trepidation, I wondered how I would deal with the poor man's need to take a piss. I certainly wasn't going to unbutton his trousers and take matters in hand to help him aim. Touching another man's junk was not something I ever wanted to do. Fortunately, there were enough nurses on hand and chamber pots nearby to accommodate bodily functions. Absent those necessities, he could just piss his pants as far as I was concerned.

As I sat with the unconscious soldier, a delectable smell floated across the ward. It was a smell I recognized from my youth: frying fish! Memories of my paternal grandmother's kitchen and its goodness came flooding back to the forefront of my consciousness. I knew that Lake Erie, the Detroit River, and Lake St. Clair at one time produced plenty of edible fish, mostly yellow perch and walleye, enough that a thriving commercial fishery once existed. I could not wait until dinner was served.

When the Officers' Mess opened, I was first in line. My hunger at that point was almost overpowering. I took a few filets of the fish, some of the vegetables that had grown in gardens outside what was left of Fort Malden, a mug of watered-down rum, and sat down to eat, oblivious to my surroundings.

My thoughts immediately went to my predicament and how I might get back to my own time. My memory of the day I jumped back to 1813 was fragmented. I remembered stacking cannon balls on the green near the Perry Memorial at sunrise – in 2017 – but nothing more until I was aroused from a stupor and given the "Hey, you!" detail by the vainglorious bastard of an officer – in 1813.

I had read plenty of science and historical fiction novels during my off-duty time and quite a few of them involved time travel. In each instance, some event or action by a character provided them access to a portal through time, either forward or backward. One that stuck in my mind involved a symbol from Greek mythology, Hecate's Wheel. In that story, the traveler traced the wheel in a particular pattern, jumping 360 years either direction in time.

A vague memory of the number 204 kept popping up, but I was not making a connection to my predicament. Was there some sort of mathematical significance to that number? I decided to find an engineer, shipwright, or artillery officer, all of whom likely would have studied advanced mathematics and mathematical theory to some degree.

Instead, I found a surveyor – another profession where advanced skills in mathematics were of paramount importance. The surveyor, Solomon Grimsby, was not a military man at all; rather, a civilian contracted by the United States Government to eventually survey the boundary between the Indiana and Michigan Territories. I would soon discover that he was well-versed in both mathematics and arithmancy, the 19th Century word for numerology.

Grimsby explained to me that there were certain numbers, called 'square pyramidal numbers,' that were purported to have mystical properties. "Though, my boy, I have never seen any confirming evidence of such properties myself," he chuckled, his extreme and well-waxed handlebar moustache twitching as if it were a living, breathing creature.

Going deep into the mathematical theory behind square pyramidal numbers, Grimsby explained the complicated formula for determining the number of objects in a square pyramid. It was a difficult concept to grasp. Never one for detailed explanations of anything outside the world of explosive ordnance disposal, my eyes glazed over as he talked.

"Lieutenant Harris, I have memorized the first dozen numbers in the sequence of square pyramidal numbers," Grimsby said, speaking as if I were in a St. John's College lecture hall full of yawning students. "They are 1… 5…14… 30… 55… 91… 140… 204 – "

My jaw dropped as I interrupted Grimsby's train of thought. "Wait… did you say 'two hundred and four', Mr. Grimsby?"

"I most certainly did," he replied.

Suddenly, it all came flooding back to me and I broke out in a cold sweat. The number 204 was that of the last sphere I placed on the pyramid of cannon balls we recovered from the bottom of Lake Erie. I now vividly remembered counting the last five balls as I placed them on the stack. I remembered the aura, the sensations, the sound, and the weakness that overcame me when the pyramid was complete.

I must have suffered some degree of situational amnesia. The memory gaps and how those gaps were slowly re-filled over time certainly fit for a situational event. It was not unlike the Post-Traumatic Stress Disorder that I had seen in hardened combat veterans who were trying to mentally separate themselves from their battlefield experiences.

As I lay in my cot that evening in 'officers' country,' I pondered Grimsby's revelations. The Hecate's Wheel story had a clear connection between forward and backward time travel, but I could not figure out how any of my actions up to this point could be reversed and take me back to 2017. Was I going to be stuck in 1813 for the rest of my natural days? My vivid dreams of this reality turned to nightmares as the hours of darkness passed towards sunrise.

10: Another Battle Looms
Late September, 1813

I had spent several near-sleepless nights, thanks to Solomon Grimsby's unintentional connection of my predicament with the number '204.' My dreams took me back to the depths of Lake Erie under the *Maumee Marauder*. I could vividly remember every flotation bag I filled with the detritus of a battle that had taken place 204 years before the dive. Strangely, though, the dreams always ended with me coming back to the surface in the midst of a raging naval battle with the *Marauder* nowhere in sight.

Recognizing that I could not fixate on the continuum of time without going completely mad, I decided that I had to make the most of my present situation. I would, as ordered by Oliver Hazard Perry himself, do my best to serve with distinction as the Executive Officer on board the *Lawrence,* which had been badly damaged in the Battle of Put-In-Bay.

The *Lawrence* was still afloat, but barely. Her masts were unstable, and she was holed just above the waterline in several places. The two captured British ships were just as badly damaged from the battle and had sustained further indignity in a storm on September 13. Thankfully, a competent shipwright from Detroit was in charge of the repairs and would remain with the *Lawrence* until the first snowfall. I was better suited to the administrative side of things and had taken full responsibility for the wounded that were now housed in the serviceable areas of the *Lawrence* and *Niagara* under the supervision of Doctors Wilcox and Smithwick. To ensure proximity to their charges, I had ordered them to be re-billeted on board the *Lawrence* instead of in the tent city ashore.

Smithwick had assumed the administrative responsibility for treating the British sick and wounded left behind as too ill or too gravely wounded to travel overland with the rapidly moving main force. Except for Smithwick, the British were now all *de facto* prisoners of war, reversing the roles they once held over the former American prisoners under the care of Doctor Wilcox.

It would be erroneous to continue with an assertion that the American doctor only treated American patients while the British doctor only treated his own countrymen. My observations showed Wilcox and Smithwick to be the consummate professionals. They didn't care at all what uniform a wounded man wore; everyone was equal in their eyes and deserved the same quality of care.

However, the sailors and soldiers were by necessity segregated by national allegiance. Tempers often flared, especially when a man who had been press-ganged into service decided to vent his frustrations. Wounded or not, punishment was necessary, and it fell to me to administer that punishment.

I knew from my own study of naval history that punishment in the pre-Civil War military could be harsh and severe, more so in the Navy than the Army. Men were flogged, denied rations, and sometimes even branded for infractions. Imposing the fear of corporal punishment was a basic tool of military discipline. My conscience would not let me lapse back to those dark times.

I decided that most minor infractions could be dealt with simply by placing the miscreant in isolation. A healthy offender would be sequestered in a secluded corner of a below-deck space while a wounded man would just be moved away from all human contact, save for myself, either of the doctors, or any of the visiting nurses we had hired from the local populace. Wounded men craved human contact, as I had seen first-hand during my own time; their recoveries often were expedited and even miraculous when they had a nearby support network of family or friends.

By the end of September, the situation aboard the *Lawrence* had settled into a routine, with recovering "walking wounded" American soldiers being released almost daily. Since the Lake Erie battle, the number of patients occupying beds and hammocks aboard the hospital ships was reduced by about half from its initial count of around 200.

The dwindling patient count had lightened my workload considerably; however, it was to be a short-lived situation. My commanding officer, the more senior Lieutenant Bradford, had taken ill with 'the bloody flux' and had to be removed to shore. For the duration of his illness, I was temporarily in command.

It was a good thing that the predicaments of the wounded had stabilized. Late on October 2, a messenger arrived from the eastern end of Lake St. Clair at the mouth of the Thames River. I quickly read the message and summoned the two doctors to my cramped quarters, which also served as a briefing room.

"Doctors, a message from General Harrison indicates that his army is in pursuit of a combined force of British regulars and Tecumseh's Confederacy. Harrison's force has skirmished with the rear guard of the retreating British under

General Procter. Both sides have sustained casualties. Under orders from General Harrison himself, we are to provide medical care to those casualties when they arrive here by wagon."

Doctor Wilcox pursed his lips, furrowed his brow, and tented his fingers at his chin before he spoke. "Sir, the wounded are not likely to survive an overland transit by wagon. It is my recommendation that either myself or Doctor Smithwick take a wagonload of supplies and two nurses to intercept the incoming wagons somewhere along the route, halt their return, triage the patients, and provide as much palliative care as we can. That will give the wounded the best chance of surviving until they reach our location."

Wilcox was clearly ahead of his time. He had already recognized the importance of evaluating and treating the severely wounded as close as possible to the front lines. "Doing so," he explained, "gives them the greatest chance of survival. A bumpy wagon ride of several miles could prove fatal."

"Agreed, Doctor Wilcox," I replied with a short nod of assent. "Which of you would like to volunteer for this assignment?"

Wilcox didn't give Smithwick a chance to respond. "I will, Lieutenant Harris. By your leave, I will take Nurses Pritchard and Shelton with me. They have proven themselves worthy and have performed admirably under very harsh battlefield conditions. They are also unmarried."

"Doctor Wilcox, please make haste with your preparations. I will provide you with the necessary letters of introduction." Inside, I was amazed at how easily I had shifted into the role of 19th Century Naval Officer. All of this now seemed to be second nature to me.

While Wilcox was assembling his supplies, the two nurses, and their bivouac equipment, Smithwick made his rounds ashore. It was during these rounds when he discovered that Lieutenant Bradford had taken a turn for the worse during the previous night and had passed away only minutes before Doctor Smithwick's arrival at the isolation tent. In his informal verbal report to me, Smithwick said that the poor man had "simply shit himself to death." In the formal military report, the cause of death would be listed as 'the bloody flux,' which was the euphemism of the day for dysentery, a more common killer of military personnel than battle wounds.

My status as temporary commanding officer just became permanent. I was now in charge of a fairly large military hospital with assets both afloat and ashore. I say 'assets', but they were really nothing more than the three damaged ships, a few tents, cots, hammocks, a field kitchen and rudimentary surgical equipment. I certainly wished I had 20th Century medical technology to support me – and my two doctors.

Doctor Wilcox and the nurses had all of their equipment loaded onto a wagon as the sun was setting over the Michigan Territory to our west. They would be ready to depart at dawn. Out of concern for their safety and knowing that there were still deserters and small bands of Native marauders roaming the area, I ordered a small armed cavalry detail to be assembled to accompany the wagon. It was a meager effort that would exhaust our resources as there were only six cavalry horses remaining in the camp around Fort Malden. I knew the cost, but also knew that without the escort, I was sending Doctor Wilcox and the two nurses into a potentially dangerous situation and possibly to their own deaths. Such was the loneliness of command.

As the medical unit prepared to depart the next morning, I took Doctor Wilcox aside. "Doctor, are you comfortable with a pistol?"

"Of course, I am, Lieutenant. I was raised in New York and lived on the frontier for quite a while. Why do you ask?"

"I feel that perhaps you should be armed, Doctor. Your escort might not be able to fully protect you," I explained.

"Perhaps I should keep the pistols hidden from the nurses?" Wilcox suggested.

"That, sir, might be a good idea. Having a concealed weapon someplace useful just might save your life!" I exclaimed.

"This is a British Army wagon," Wilcox said, "and they always build a hidden compartment immediately below the driver's seat. It is just large enough to hold two pistols and a bag or two of coins."

"A good observation, Doctor Wilcox," I replied.

"We also have a reasonable supply of laudanum and whiskey. Both are often necessary to ease a man's suffering, and a large dose of laudanum can make an amputation much easier to perform," Wilcox also explained.

The cook had prepared several parcels of non-perishable food like hardtack and jerky. The hardtack always tasted like cardboard and the jerky had the texture of well-worn shoe leather. Not exactly culinary delights, but the departing medical party would not starve. The cook had also put by a small barrel of salted walleye from Lake Saint Clair. That, I realized, would taste much better than the alternatives. The cook had also managed to find several dozen apples from somewhere across the river in the Michigan Territory.

I made sure of one other small detail that might ensure the unimpeded movement of the medical team I was sending out into the wild. They had to travel under a white flag of truce. At least as far as military encounters of the early 19th Century were concerned, persons moving under a white flag were declaring themselves noncombatants. Whether or not the flag would be honored by an enemy force was entirely discretionary. They could still be shot on sight. I had to trust their safety to the code of conduct of the period.

11: Branches in the Tree
Put-in-Bay, October 1, 2017

Tensions between Jacqui and James Wilcox had increased since the discovery that Marcus Harris was missing. Sean Hagerty, too, was perplexed that there was no sign of his friend, nor had any remains been discovered. Sure, there were currents in Lake Erie that could have carried Marcus's body away from South Bass Island, but that was unlikely without the body floating to the surface and being discovered.

For her part, Jacqui Wilcox was obsessed with the dashing Navy retiree. She dreamed of him when she was asleep; she fantasized about him when she was awake. She even thought of and saw Marcus Harris's face the few times she and James had sex after Marcus's disappearance a month earlier.

"Having sex, that's it exactly. It's just sex, not lovemaking," she would rationalize to herself. *"I enjoy it much more when I replace James with Marcus in my mind."*

Her mind quickly strayed to her seeing Marcus changing into his wetsuit the day of their first dive. Broad shoulders, well-defined pectoral muscles, six-pack abs, bulging biceps, and next to no body hair, except for that fine line between his navel and… well….

Then there was his deep voice… with just a trace of a southern drawl in his speech in spite of his southeastern Michigan origin. Marcus was definitely more physically appealing than the now-paunchy James.

"I have to stop thinking about Marcus this way," she repeatedly told herself, but the fantasy of touching him, being close enough to smell him, was almost more than she could handle.

James Wilcox, on the other hand, was laser-focused on his research, but had gone down the rabbit hole of genealogy, ignoring just about everything else going on around him, including Jacqui's unmistakable attempts to get his attention. He was now wondering if Marcus might have a distant relative nearby who would have taken him in. Instead of finding more information about the Marcus Harris of 2017, James ended up making a couple of unusual discoveries from historical records over 200 years in the past.

He already knew about Doctor Stephen Wilcox and the War of 1812, at least that the doctor existed as an ancestor. Searching through several online databases of military and genealogical records, James stumbled across what looked to be scanned notes from Stephen Wilcox's case books and personal journals starting about the time Doctor Wilcox was taken prisoner in the Battle of Frenchtown. As he quickly clicked through a scanned journal, one entry in particular jumped out at him:

*"**October 12, 1813:** I returned to Fort Malden and gave a full report to Lieutenant Marcus Harris."*

James stopped and rubbed his eyes. "I must be over-tired or something, I could swear that entry said 'Marcus Harris,'" he mumbled in a voice barely above a whisper. He had to keep reading.

*"**October 12, 1813:** I returned to Fort Malden and gave a full report to the commander, Lieutenant Marcus Harris. I described how we had treated the wounded left in the wake of General Harrison's advance and General Procter's retreat. I could not immediately convey the details of Tecumseh's death nor the wounds of revenge that had been inflicted on the bodies of the Native fighters. They were just too horrific to describe, at least while stone cold sober. A few glasses of wine later, my tongue loosened, and I was able to recount most of my experiences. The horrors of the mutilations defied any sense of humanity: watching a man bleed to death from his genital area is not something I will*

ever forget. The man, I think he was an Indian, had been left behind for dead and I believe he was set upon by a River Raisin survivor who inflicted the mutilation."

Marcus Harris… Stephen Wilcox… together. Was it a coincidence or something else entirely? James was going to try to find out.

12: Retreat, Defeat, and Carnage
Beginning on October 2, 1813

My deployed medical team quickly and unexpectedly caught up with Major General Harrison's rear guard. The American force was strung out along the whole southern shore of Lake Saint Clair because of the rapid advance and near-constant encounters with British stragglers and Natives from Tecumseh's disintegrating confederation. The British stragglers, Doctor Wilcox would later report, were under-nourished, having been on half rations for over a week.

Wilcox was delayed by the necessity of caring for the sick and wounded along the way. As much as he could, Wilcox stuck to the intent of his orders and kept the team moving towards Chatham, another twenty miles west the mouth of the Thames. They arrived there on the evening of October 4.

It was at Chatham that the numerically superior American force skirmished briefly with Tecumseh's fighters. The engagements were intended to slow the advance of the Americans, but the Natives were quickly overwhelmed. The overall British situation was made worse by the last of their supply boats running aground with the last of their food and reserve ammunition.

Just after dawn on October 5, Procter ordered his forces to abandon their camp, even leaving their breakfast behind. It was a typical Procter tactic: to run away before being overwhelmed rather than standing and fighting. He had abandoned Fort Malden under similar circumstances.

I learned later that the so-called "Battle of the Thames" really was not much of a battle at all. It transpired as just a half-hearted effort by the exhausted and hungry British regulars to mount a defense. General Procter himself had already fled the battlefield and the rag-tag remnants of his army quickly laid down their arms and surrendered.

With the main British force now disengaged, only Tecumseh and his warriors were left in the fight. Mounted Kentucky riflemen, led by Colonel James Johnson, charged into the midst of Tecumseh's fighters and were briefly repelled by a volley of musket fire. In the end, though, Tecumseh himself lay dead. With that news quickly spreading, the Native resistance quickly dissolved.

Doctor Wilcox also reported to me that there were survivors of the River Raisin incident among the American forces. These men, from both Michigan Territory and Kentucky, were hell-bent on revenge for the atrocities inflicted on their comrades-in-arms ten months earlier. The dead and dying Natives were subjected to scalping, flaying, and other mutilation by the enraged militiamen seeking souvenirs of their conquest.

Doctor Wilcox returned to Fort Malden about a week after the battle. The normally talkative Wilcox was unusually sullen and taciturn. Not even Doctor Smithwick could elicit more than a few syllables from his friend. It took some coaxing from me before Wilcox would respond. With several glasses of wine in his belly, he finally felt comfortable enough to open up about his adventure.

"Lieutenant Harris," Wilcox began, "If I could have gotten the names of the men responsible for the desecration of those bodies, I would gladly have turned them over to you. It is unconscionable that supposedly civilized men could have inflicted such atrocities on other human beings. It doesn't matter to me that they were tribesmen loyal to Tecumseh; they were still men. Still human beings."

"Would you recognize any of them on sight?" I asked, hoping that he would be able to do so.

"That, Lieutenant, is what troubles me. The perpetrators, being militiamen and on foot, were in backwoods garb and fully bearded. Colonel Johnson's cavalry recognized they had the victory and honorably quit the field once Tecumseh was dead and his warriors dispersed. The men of Johnson's cavalry were all in uniform and clean-shaven. They were definitely not the culprits."

Now relaxed and loquacious, Wilcox spent the next couple of hours providing vivid details of his mission. He did tell me that he was surprised by the small number of wounded. This he attributed to the wooded terrain and the inaccuracy of the British "Brown Bess" smoothbore muskets beyond 100 yards. I surmised that the retreating British were firing at Harrison's forces well outside that effective range, significantly reducing both the velocity and force of the projectile before it had the opportunity to penetrate human flesh.

This was the first time I had been the inquisitor in the post-mortem of a military engagement. In my time, I was usually on the other side of the table, reporting on the engagement from a combatant's point of view. Each death in a surgical operation – and the reason for it – had to be justified and documented. Warfare in the 19th Century was completely different and I was astounded by the uncaring and inhumane treatment of the enemy. Eventually, I moved the conversation in another direction.

"How did the two nurses perform?" I asked.

"They conducted themselves admirably and did not flinch from the horrors of war," Wilcox said as he waxed into eloquence.

"Boy, this guy would be right at home as a bureaucrat in my time," I thought. *"He'll put me to sleep if I listen for too long."*

"Nurses Shelton and Pritchard were assets to our efforts, giving aid and comfort to the wounded, even praying with them if they asked," said Wilcox. "We had no chaplain, and Nurse Shelton in particular, as a former nun in the Daughters of Charity order, was quite well suited to caring for the needs of the faithful, Roman Catholic or not."

After taking Wilcox's detailed statement, I called for Doctor Smithwick to join us as we opened a second bottle of wine. Smithwick instinctively knew that his friend's mental state would be precarious and did his best to keep the conversation light and away from the horrors of war.

"Stephen, what do you plan to do when the war is over?" Smithwick asked.

"I am not entirely certain, Simon. I can see myself as a small-town physician somewhere in either the Michigan Territory or perhaps in northwestern Ohio. Taking care of farmers' injuries and birthing their children seems like an idyllic life. I know I gave that up in New York, but it seemed like the right thing to do at the time," Wilcox explained. "What about you, Simon?"

"I do not wish to return to England and likely will remain here in Canada," Smithwick responded. "Who knows, I might even find myself a wife!" I filed that away in my memory; a man normally didn't make such a statement unless he had the intent – and a potential bride – in mind. I wondered if he might have romantic intentions towards one of our nurses.

Wilcox kept the conversation going. "I cannot see myself as a married man. I like being independent and having only my patients relying on me. Adding a wife and probably children to my life would just complicate things. I value simplicity," he said emphatically.

"Lieutenant? Do you have plans after the war is over?" Smithwick asked.

I knew I had to choose my next words carefully. My knowledge of the social conditions and mores of the day was limited. I wanted to avoid at all costs any chance of an egregious error in my interpretations of facts as I understood them to be.

Another thing complicating my situation was that I grew up in the area between Detroit and Toledo. In 1813, the area could not have been much more than a few farms in the wilderness that were quickly encroaching on Native American lands. I had been taught precious little in high school history classes about the region, other than that white settlers displaced most of the Natives by the 1830s, which were still two decades in the future. In fact, most high school curricula for that area emphasized that George Armstrong Custer was raised in Monroe – and that he graduated from West Point at the bottom of his class.

Could I quickly come up with a plausible life story? It had to be both believable and sustainable. The doctors would surely ask if I had a wife and family and how I came to be the acting commander of the Fort Malden hospital. They would ask about my military career. The list of questions they *could* ask was mind-boggling. Was I up to the challenge? I was in a pickle, and I knew it. I had to handle my response as I would a combat interrogation.

Crafting my story in my head, I stared into my wine goblet for what seemed like hours. I finally decided that it would be best to have come from someplace south of the Great Lakes and far away from New York. Smithwick, unless he had intimate knowledge of U.S. geography, would not be able to challenge any of my assertions and I had already surmised that Wilcox's knowledge was geographically limited as well. He knew New York and perhaps Pennsylvania but seemed to have a limited awareness of anything south of Philadelphia.

It might have been easier to explain my Navy connection through Annapolis and I had originally intended to craft my story around the United States Naval Academy, Just as I was ready to speak, a mental alarm bell went off in my head: the Naval Academy was not established until 1845. Every student of naval history, both officer and enlisted, should know that date. The Annapolis of 1813 was little more than a backwater town with a thriving seafood industry, its connection to the importation of slaves having dwindled since the 1740s. *Too many unknowns,* I thought to myself.

As if I had been struck by lightning, Baltimore loomed large as a plausible location of my origin. In 1813, was as cosmopolitan as any other East Coast city. It was also large enough that an individual could maintain anonymity. Any facts I created would not be challenged. As I had been taught in my time, if you craft a cover story, convey as few details as possible; more details to remember means more chances of screwing up the story and getting caught in a lie..

"Gentlemen, I hail from Maryland, near Baltimore," I began, pausing for effect after each fact, "and spent my time as a waterman in the northern Chesapeake Bay."

"So far, so good," I thought, *"they were buying it."*

"I've never been to Baltimore," Wilcox said. "What's the city like? I've read plenty in the New York newspapers about escaped slaves coming north from Virginia, through Maryland, and being pursued by bounty hunters." His tone was puzzling to me; it sounded almost rehearsed.

"I don't know for sure about any of that," I replied. "There would be Black – " *"Wait a minute… that term wasn't widely used until the 1960s…"* " – Negro watermen from time to time, but I never knew if they were slaves or freedmen." *"Whew, that was close!"* "I spent my time from before dawn until dusk out on the water. In the summer, we would fish and catch crabs. In the winter, we dredged for oysters. It was a boring, demanding life."

That turned the conversation away from me and left Wilcox and Smithwick comparing clinical notes about procedures Wilcox had performed in the field. From their conversation, I learned more about 19th Century amputations and gunshot wounds than I ever wanted to know. They both also lamented that infection, gangrene, and disease took more lives than the wounds themselves.

I knew Wilcox was ahead of his time with sanitary and antiseptic procedures and I was puzzled that he might have first-hand knowledge of medicine that had not yet been developed. Then it occurred to me: could he, too, have come to 1813 from another time? I would just have to find out. But how?

13: Revelations
Mid-October, 1813

My military training had also included battlefield reconnaissance, a skill that was easily applied to my present situation. I would observe, I would memorize. I would note inconsistencies that I could later exploit.

Doctor Smithwick was behaving appropriately for a man of his time. On the other hand, there was something about Wilcox that didn't ring true. Closer observation was needed. I had to find out more about the mysterious Doctor Stephen Wilcox.

The only way I was going to find out more information than what Wilcox was telling me in our daily meetings was to surreptitiously access his clinical notes or his journals. He prided himself in keeping those notes since his time as a prisoner of war and now as a military surgeon; I knew they would be complete.

A new wave of dysentery was making its way through the hospital camp. I felt it best to separate the two doctors, one ashore and one remaining aboard the *Lawrence*, until the daily number of new cases trended downward. The last thing I wanted was for both doctors to become ill at the same time, which was a near certainty as they shared adjacent quarters on the *Lawrence* one deck immediately below my own.

After a short deliberation, I decided that it would be Wilcox who would remain ashore as I knew he had just started both a new clinical record and a new journal. He was likely to leave his older volumes behind in his quarters on the *Lawrence,* sending for them only if they were needed. This might be my opportunity.

Because Wilcox and Smithwick occupied adjacent quarters, I would need to time my entry into Wilcox's cabin such that Smithwick was engaged in patient care elsewhere on the ship. I knew that he would spend at least an hour for sick call, starting with the 0800 watch. After that, he would compile his notes and transcribe the binnacle list of sailors physically unable to perform their duties.

As Commanding Officer, even in my "acting" role, I enjoyed certain privileges that others did not. I could in most cases conduct searches of living quarters for contraband or evidence of wrongdoing. I could use that to my advantage, but the downside would be that I was jeopardizing my relationship with the two doctors. It was certainly something I would have to wrestle with.

Two days (and two near-sleepless nights) later, I had made my decision. I would go into Doctor Wilcox's quarters on board the *Lawrence* and search for contraband. What constituted contraband was mine alone to define.

I quietly entered Doctor Wilcox's quarters just after 8 a.m. There was precious little space for much other than his wardrobe and journals; the quarters were spartan and largely devoid of personal effects. After a very brief search, I discovered his notes in a well-made portmanteau that was lockable but unlocked. Wilcox's obsession with detail and organization made it easy to find the first volume of his case files. I quickly thumbed through it until I found something a little out of the ordinary.

*"**December 15, 1812:** A man returning from leave complained of a burning sensation when he urinates. I suspect he had visited a brothel and come back with a case of gonorrhea. He had engaged in one of the common treatments of the day, clapping his penis between his hands. I believe this is where the euphemism "the clap" came from.*

Then there was a statement in Latin. Seeing that language, I was transported back to my Latin classes in the Catholic school. Sister Mary Grace and her ever-present ruler. The whacks across the back of my left hand; I was right-handed and she always spared the miscreant's writing hand to preserve good penmanship. I began to shudder, clenching and unclenching my left hand as the memory of the pain came flooding back. I unconsciously massaged my left hand with my right to alleviate the remembered, phantom pain and I closed my eyes to blot out the vision of Sister Mary Grace's evil and almost maniacal grin as she meted out her punishment.

My mind now clear, I pressed on with the Latin: *"Medicina moderna cum antibioticis hoc circiter septimana samaret."* Wilcox was wishing for 'modern medicne' with antibiotics! A week's treatment was all that his patient would need.

Wilcox *was* from another time, just like me! Antibiotics would not be discovered for another 115 years. He knew they were coming, lamented their absence, and hid his knowledge in a Latin entry in his case book. I had to confront Doctor Wilcox, but it needed to be in a very private and secluded location away from the ship and Fort Malden.

14: Confrontation
Mid-October, 1813

The dysentery outbreak took about ten days to subside before Doctor Wilcox felt it would be safe for him to return to the *Lawrence* and his quarters. I knew that he would then spend several hours each day updating his leather-bound case books as all he had ashore was loose paper. Wilcox was meticulous and preferred that his notes be in bound portfolios, not left to scatter to the wind. After his notes were transcribed, the original copies would be burned.

With Wilcox back on board, I immediately set up a meeting with him, Doctor Smithwick, and myself. My purported goal for the meeting was to go over the care of our patients, supply needs, and plans for the upcoming winter, which came early in this part of North America. We had to allow for shelter, clothing, and sanitation to get us through the freezing temperatures that started as early as November.

Doctor Wilcox, I knew, would be focused on sanitation. He would probably insist that winter latrines be dug ahead of time and not postponed until they were actually needed. This might be my opportunity to go ashore with him to both lay out the new latrine sites and to discuss my discovery from his medical journals. He didn't let me down.

"Lieutenant Harris, please understand that the ground will be frozen a couple of feet down by Christmas and asking the men to dig through the frozen turf would be unreasonable."

"What do you suggest, Doctor Wilcox?" I countered.

"Let me take you ashore and show you where I recommend the winter latrines be dug," he replied. "Each one has to be further away from our water supply than the last. We cannot risk another outbreak of dysentery in the middle of the winter when everyone is in close quarters and huddled around a warming fire."

"Hmm..." I thought, *"he didn't call it 'bloody flux' like they did back then... now."*

"Very well. We will go ashore as soon as this meeting is adjourned," I agreed. He was predictable, for sure. I don't think he even realized that I was playing him like a fiddle.

Doctor Smithwick largely echoed Wilcox's observations throughout the meeting. Of the two, Smithwick was the most introverted and least independent. He tended to go along with whatever Wilcox proposed. I was worried that Smithwick was starting to show the signs of depression, 'melancholy' they called it back then, and his mental health could deteriorate further during the bleakness of winter.

After two hours, Wilcox and I were ready to go ashore. The *Lawrence* was on the eastern side of the Detroit River adjacent to Fort Malden, so any latrine system would have to be dug progressively further east. Thankfully, the area was largely uninhabited, and we would be able to absorb the land into the military-controlled area around Fort Malden.

Wilcox had other ideas. He wanted to use the western side of the river as well and suggested that the *Lawrence* be moved to the docks on the Detroit side. He noted that our patients were, for the time being, almost equally divided between the hospital ashore and the berths aboard the *Lawrence*.

"Splitting the latrine system on either side of the river," he explained, "would ease the burden on a single location. It might be harder to maintain in the long run, but the river is not wide, the current is relatively slow, and it freezes pretty solidly in the winter. It will easily support a man walking across the ice, and perhaps even a team of horses pulling a lightly loaded wagon."

"Being from Maryland, I've never encountered ice that would support a man, much less a team and a wagon," I said, more to emphasize my purported origins than anything else.

"When I was interned at Fort Malden as a prisoner of war last winter, the Natives would come across the river with food and supplies for the British garrison. I watched how easily they made the crossing," Wilcox said.

"What if the river doesn't freeze like you expect it to?" I asked.

"We will just have to deal with that situation if it presents itself," Wilcox replied. "We still have most of the rowboats from the battle last month. They are heavy enough to break through thinner ice and be used as ferries if necessary."

"Let's look at the latrine sites to the east first," I said, trying to get the conversation focused again on why we were ashore.

To mark the recommended sites, I carried a knapsack filled with sharpened stakes. The flat opposite end of each stake had been dipped in red dye for visibility. They were roughly three feet long and would only serve as temporary markers if the snow became too deep. Wilcox carried the maul we would use to drive the stakes into the ground and already had a plan to place more permanent location markers before the first snowfall. We also carried the remnants of a red British army tunic torn into strips; we would affix these to tree branches overhanging a prospective latrine location.

After staking the first location, I decided that we were far enough from the *Lawrence* and Fort Malden that we would not be overheard. Feigning thirst, I sat down on a log, pulled the cork stopper from my wooden canteen, and took a long sip. Doctor Wilcox did the same from his own.

We tended to dispense with formalities when away from the confines of the hospital and fell easily into casual conversation. It was normally "Doctor" or "Lieutenant" when in the presence of others – but in private one-on-one settings, it was "Stephen" and "Marcus." I opened the dialog but remained cautious.

"Stephen, I am curious… While you were ashore dealing with the dysentery… bloody flux outbreak, I had a need to enter your quarters on the Lawrence and look through some of your personal effects and luggage.– "

Wilcox interrupted, "What was the need for you to enter my quarters?" His tone was indignant.

"As the commanding officer, it is within my authority and prerogative to enter the quarters of anyone under my command," I said in defense of my actions. "We were trying to determine the source of a noxious odor, perhaps a decomposing rat, that increased when I got close to your quarters. Once inside, I opened your portmanteau to inspect it for vermin."

"Rats? In my quarters? Surely, you jest!" he responded. Rats seemed to be everywhere on the *Lawrence*; they were so pervasive that we kept a small army of felines on board as well.

I couldn't tell if this reply was hostile or playfully sarcastic. I had to press on with my explanation. The story was, in my opinion, believable and appropriate for the living arrangements we shared on our floating hospital.

"Rats seem to like things made of fine leather, so I lifted several of your clinical portfolios from the portmanteau and opened the first volume. I couldn't help but noticing your description of a soldier's affliction with a venereal disease." *Had I just tipped my hand?* I thought to myself. *Was that a term that was even used in 1813?*

"Oh, that…" Wilcox responded. "The current treatment is quite comical, in my opinion." He was stifling a laugh as he spoke. "It was how it came to be called 'the clap'."

"You can spare me the details for now, Stephen." I recognized that it was time for me to pounce. "What about that Latin statement you wrote? Was that just doctor talk? My Latin may be a little rusty, but I did understand that you were wishing for 'modern medicine' and 'antibiotics' to help the poor man."

Wilcox's eyes grew wide in shock, and I paused to let the gravity of the moment sink in. I think he suddenly realized that he was no longer alone as a transplant from the 20th Century.

I decided that the time was right to just come clean and share my story. "Stephen, I was brought here from the year 2017. I was supposed to be a re-enactor for a commemoration of the Battle of Lake Erie. Before the celebration, I had spent the previous week in a diving expedition to recover over 200 cannonballs from the battle.

"I was stacking the cannonballs into a pyramid for display, 204 of them to be exact, and when I was about to place the final one at the apex, the ground vibrated like an earthquake tremor and I felt displaced, out of sorts, like I was no longer in control of my own movements. Forces inside the stack of cannonballs pulled me closer and as I added the last one. The next thing I knew, I was being yelled at by a naval officer getting ready to do battle against the British Lake Erie fleet."

"Oh… my… God…" Wilcox moaned as he covered his now-ashen face with his hands. It took a few moments for him to regain his composure before speaking again, "I came from 1992 and how I got here is a mystery and certainly not as exciting as your story."

"Do tell," I answered, "perhaps we can figure it out together."

"I was in New Haven, Connecticut, doing some genealogical research. I knew my family tree had its roots there, despite me being from upstate. Ever hear of Oswego, at the eastern end of Lake Ontario?"

"Yes. There is a university there," I answered.

"I was the campus physician," Wilcox explained. "Anyway, we were still on winter break, and I took advantage of the time to visit New Haven and an old church where I had heard there was an archive of genealogical information going back to the 1600s. My family on both sides is connected to New Haven."

"Interesting," I said more as an acknowledgement that I was still listening than anything else.

Wilcox continued, "The pastor gave me access to the crypt beneath the church. It was not an easy descent, more of a ladder, really, than stairs." He paused for a moment to collect his thoughts. "The crypt itself was pitch-black and the only light was from the bulb at the top of the stairs. Before I started down, the pastor told me that I should light the candles in the wall sconces opposite the base of the ladder, even though I had a very powerful flashlight."

"That sounds odd," I commented. "Why would he insist on using the candles instead of a flashlight?"

"It wasn't supposed to be an 'instead of.' He made it clear that it was 'in addition to' the light I carried," Wilcox replied. "It would all become clear in a few minutes, I would soon learn."

'What do you mean?" I asked. Wilcox was a master storyteller and had a knack for building suspense as he spoke.

Wilcox cocked his head to one side like an inquisitive canine before continuing, "I lit the candles and started shuffling through a stack of very old papers on the… I guess it was an old stone altar. It didn't take me long to find what I was looking for."

"What was that?" I asked.

"The baptismal record from 1631… my eleventh great-grandmother, Dorcas Parham Pinkerton," he answered. "She married a man named Jonas Starbuck sometime around

1660. I am pretty sure, but can't confirm it, that she was married at least once before."

"I am surprised that the papers had survived almost three hundred years," I commented.

"I can't explain it, either," Wilcox parried, "but when I touched Jonas Starbuck's name on the paper, strange things started to happen.

"Such as?" I was now very curious.

"First, the candles started sputtering as if whey were in a strong wind," Wilcox explained. "I felt compelled to touch a drawing on the wall opposite the staircase. It was a circle with a maze of some kind superimposed inside it."

He continued, "I traced the outer path of the maze with my finger and for some reason stopped at the very bottom. Try as I might, my finger would not go from the bottom dead center back to the top. I was stuck. In limbo. No amount of willfulness on my part would make my finger move."

"Which direction did you trace the circle? Clockwise or counterclockwise?" I asked.

"Counterclockwise. Backwards for a clock. With my finger at the bottom, the candles spluttered again, then they went out completely. I think I might have lost consciousness or was completely disoriented. It took some time for me to gather my wits about me, as I thought I was stuck in a bad dream. Still not totally aware of time or place, I suddenly came to the realization that I was completely naked. The only thing connecting me to the past… future… was my medical bag.""

"That is so bizarre," I replied. "I was transported to this time and was in full military uniform when I arrived. I certainly wasn't naked. Maybe it had to do with the fact that I was already planning to be a re-enactor at a commemoration of the Battle of Lake Erie and my uniform was appropriate for the time."

Wilcox considered what I had just said. "So, there was a connection between your past… uhh… your 'before' and right now, something you did?"

"It seems so," I replied. "I think it was the cannonballs in my case. In yours, I think the circle maze must be the connection. Can you try to draw the circle for me?"

It took Wilcox about fifteen minutes to draw a facsimile of what he had seen. I recognized it almost instantly as 'Hecate's Wheel.' I was a fan of Greek mythology in my younger years but did not recall any connection to Hecate's Wheel and legends of time travel.

At first, we were both stumped. Our situations and the catalyst for our jumps backward in time were completely different. Mine seemed to have something to do with the aggregate power of a sphere and a pyramid, but Stephen's predicament was much more of a mystery.

Then it hit me: the bottom dead center of Hecate's Wheel was 180 degrees from the top, where he had started tracing his finger. 1992 back to 1812 was 180 years. It was as if a lightbulb had exploded in my brain. It *was* the circle after all!

"Stephen, that circle, Hecate's Wheel, is your connection to the future… uhh… your… time. You said your hand could not go any further around than half the circumference. That coincides with the number of years you jumped back."

Wilcox looked at me with a furrowed brow. I could see that he was wrestling with what I had just said, but I don't think he fully comprehended its gravity.

"Stephen, do you remember *where* you found yourself naked?" I asked.

"I think it was somewhere along the shore of Lake Erie, on the southern side, in Ohio, I think," he answered, the uncertainty in his voice was clear.

"What were you wearing in the church basement?" I inquired.

"I think I was wearing khakis and a pink polo shirt," Stephen replied.

"Hmm… In my case, I was already dressed in period costume. That could explain why I wasn't left naked in the middle of a very crowded area. You, on the other hand, would have arrived in attire that was completely inappropriate for the period. I think that might be why you ended up naked: khaki and pink polyester didn't exist in 1812," I offered as a potential explanation.

"It wasn't long before I was found by a band of Cherokee tribesmen heading west, intent on reaching the Mississippi River and heading south to join General Andrew Jackson and the Tennessee militia," Stephen said. "They gave me clothing and food, then turned me over to an American army regiment that was heading towards Frenchtown.

"I told the regimental commander that I was a surgeon who had been separated from his militia company in the wilds of Ohio. His own regiment was without a surgeon, so I signed his muster roll; it was a better option than being left behind with no means of survival. That's how I ended up treating the men wounded in the River Raisin battle."

"So, you really didn't join the army on your own in New York?" It was more of a statement than a question I was posing.

"Actually, it was more like I was absorbed by the Army in the fall of 1812, then spent most of the winter in camp before the River Raisin battle," he said with a wry smile.

"This whole thing, our arrivals here during this war, is one of the most bizarre circumstances I have ever encountered," I said as I shook my head. "We have to figure out how to get back to our own time."

Wilcox stroked his chin pensively for a few moments before beginning a soliloquy. "Marcus, I may not want to go back. I've found a purpose here, something that was lacking in my existence in 1992. Sure, I miss the medical technology of the 20th Century, which I am sure advanced even further by your time in 2017, but there's something to be said for saving lives with your bare hands, with using your knowledge from... the future... to heal the sick and wounded. It just would not be the same to go back to Oswego State University and spend my days doing nothing more than prescribing antibiotics and birth control pills. I feel like I belong here, in 1813, and really don't want to put any effort into finding my way back."

"I see," I said, but actually I didn't. "Personally, I want to get back to 2017 as quickly as I can. I retired from the Navy to get out of all of the survival and combat stuff – and I am going to say that I have probably seen as much war as you have. Enough is enough. I want to go home, back to my own time."

"Marcus, there's one other thing," Stephen said solemnly. "When you sent us east to follow General Harrison, Nurse Elizabeth… Lizzie… Pritchard and I became fast friends. I didn't have a wife in 1992 and never really felt the need to marry. It's different now. Surviving in this time takes skill. It takes perseverance. It takes courage. It takes someone to share it with."

I understood his dilemma: meeting the right woman changes a man, down to his very core. He wants nothing more than to be with her. To share things with her. To procreate with her. Once he finds that woman, nothing else matters.

"So, are you intent on… what do they say now, courting?" I asked.

"Yes, I do, Marcus, but I am not familiar with the customs of this time." Wilcox continued, "I will have to ask Simon Smithwick for help. He's sweet on the other nurse, Christina

Shelton. I think they have been having secret trysts for quite some time. I overheard her and Lizzie talking about him in the still of the night when we were camped. I don't think they were aware that I was listening."

"Interesting," I thought to myself, *"here I was, the Commanding Officer, and had no clue that romance was blooming right under my nose."*

Returning focus to the task at hand, I changed the subject. "Stephen, have we marked out enough latrine locations to get us through the winter?"

"Yes, we have," he replied, "but I still want us to mark the west side of the river as well. That's a task for tomorrow."

15: Down the Rabbit Holes of Research
November – December 2017

James Wilcox was now completely consumed by his research. He ate little, slept even less, and was occasionally so engaged as to be totally unaware of the time or his surroundings. If he lost internet connectivity for any reason or for any longer than a couple of minutes, his rage could be explosive. It was in those times that Jacqui seriously considered leaving him.

To separate herself from her husband's enraged tirades, Jacqui began spending more and more time away from the B&B. There was very little to do on South Bass Island and in Put-in-Bay outside of tourist and fishing season; the winter population dwindled down to the bare minimum after Thanksgiving. There were so few people on South Bass Island in the depths of winter that the island's police department didn't even patrol. Instead, they made periodic telephone calls, "welfare checks" they called them, to be sure that the overwinter residents were still alive.

In winter, the only safe ways on or off the island were via single-engine airplanes or helicopters; the take-offs and landings were always treacherous in winter crosswinds. For an extreme emergency, snowmobiles could attempt ice crossings to the mainland, but this practice was generally frowned upon by the Ottawa County authorities as risky and unsafe; Lake Erie ice was unstable even during the deepest freezes. "Such crossings should only be attempted in matters of life or death," their warning literature proclaimed. "We will not come out onto the ice to rescue you, and you cross at your own risk."

By Christmas of 2017, the southwestern corner of Lake Erie and the waters around South Bass Island were sufficiently frozen that a person could walk on the ice. However, it was still not strong enough to support the weight of a snowmobile. Meanwhile, the nearest land with road access was Catawba Island, three miles due south. Catawba was an island in name only; it was really a peninsula that jutted out into the lake, providing easy ferry access to South Bass Island during tourist season.

Jacqui wondered if the ice was already solid enough across that three-mile stretch of open water to support her weight. She had to get off the island or go absolutely mad. James was neglecting her and his vitriolic tirades were getting worse. There were no overwinter women in whom she could confide, and even the pastor of the island's only church moved back to Port Clinton during the winter. In the summer, his nondenominational open-air services were usually well-attended.

Flying in either a single-engine plane or helicopter was out of the question. Her name would have to be declared on the flight plan and manifest; it was her goal to covertly escape the confines of the island and disappear. She gambled that James wouldn't immediately notice her absence; she would use that time to get as far away as possible.

Jacqui decided to wait until a foolhardy snowmobiler made a successful crossing from Catawba Island on the ice. She was taking a bold step leaving James, which was risky enough. The danger of crossing the ice on her own without knowledge of previous crossings was more than she was willing to assume.

She didn't have to wait too long. Just after Christmas, she was on the southeast shore near the airstrip, wistfully contemplating her escape, when a lone snowmobiler barreled across the ice from Catawba Island. As the snowmobile approached, Jacqui began to wave her arms frantically; she wanted to attract the operator's attention and find out how the transit had been.

Pulling up on the beach next to Jacqui, the snowmobiler removed his helmet. "Good afternoon, ma'am. I saw you waving and decided to investigate. Is something the matter?"

Jacqui didn't reply immediately; she wanted to be sure her words were carefully chosen so as not to tip her hand. She also wanted to give a little hint of flirtation. "Nothing is the matter. Nothing at all." She could feel a blush rising into her cheeks. "It isn't every day that someone even attempts that crossing, much less makes it. Were you sure the ice was safe before you set out from Catawba? You did come from Catawba Island, didn't you?"

"Well, it's like this…" the early thirty-something man began to explain, "My college buddies from the University of Toledo, the ones studying meteorology, believed the recent cold snap had allowed the ice to get thick enough to support the weight of a grown man plus a snowmobile – as long as they were moving at a moderate speed. You see, ma'am, the combined weight –"

Jacqui interrupted with an indignant tone, "Young man, you can stop 'mansplaining' all of that to me. As you should be able to clearly see, I wasn't born yesterday. I know about the physics and the effects of speed on weight distribution. I went to college, too!"

"My apologies, ma'am. I didn't mean to offend," he countered. "I did notice that the ice seemed unusually smooth, quite an anomaly for Lake Erie. The ice is usually very active and piles up against a downwind shoreline. With the ice piles, it would be almost impossible for a snowmobile to cross like I just did."

After another tense pause, Jacqui extended her right hand and introduced herself. "I'm Jacqui Wilcox. I live here on South Bass Island. Now can you please stop calling me 'ma'am'?"

"Pleased to meet you, Mrs. – it is 'Mrs.', isn't it? Wilcox." Jacqui nodded affirmatively, pursing her lips as she did. "My name is Charles Gordon Bruce. I am a resident post-doctoral researcher at the University of Toledo."

"Won't you come to my Bed and Breakfast for a cup of coffee and a hot meal?" Jacqui asked.

"That would be wonderful," Charles replied. "My cold weather gear is usually quite adequate, but I think I have been sweating… nervous sweat… and I am beginning to chill."

"Follow me," Jacqui said with a wink and a twinkle in her eye. "Our B&B is only about a half mile away. Your machine will be safe here; just take the key with you."

Charles followed, wondering if he was about to be seduced by a cougar. Her demeanor and the flirtatious glances all suggested that Jacqui Wilcox was a lonely woman in need of attention. He just wasn't sure what kind.

Once they were inside the warm kitchen of the B&B, Jacqui hollered upstairs to her husband. "James, we have a visitor. Come down and be sociable, won't you?"

James's response was less than hospitable and laden with expletives. In his diatribe, he made it quite clear that he not only had no intention of coming downstairs to meet the visitor, but that he was angry at being interrupted. Put somewhat politely, James's response equated to an unequivocal "not just no, but hell, no!"

"Charles, do sit down," Jacqui pleaded. She had ignored her husband's outburst as best she could, sidestepping its venom and viciousness as best she could.

For his part, Charles Gordon Bruce was becoming more and more nervous with each passing minute. He sensed that the tension between the couple was on the verge of becoming much more than just words and had no desire to be caught in the middle of a marital squabble. On the other hand, he did appreciate Jacqui's hospitality. *"After all, it was a very cold crossing,"* he thought to himself.

"Charles, would you like some soup? I've had a stockpot of ham and vegetable soup simmering all day. It should be quite tasty by now," Jacqui asked.

"That would be wonderful, Mrs. Wilcox."

"I told you to call me 'Jacqui', please?" she countered. "How do you take your coffee, Charles?"

"Black, no sugar, please." He'd been drinking his coffee black ever since he could remember. He had fond memories of cold mornings in duck blinds with his father and the one thermos they carried was always filled with piping-hot black coffee.

"Coming right up," Jacqui said gleefully. It had been weeks, maybe even since Marcus's disappearance months earlier, since she had heard a kind, appreciative word from any man.

For the next hour, Jacqui fawned over Charles Gordon Bruce. Her syrupy-sweet attention was almost more than he could tolerate. He sensed that she wanted something from him; he just wasn't sure what it was.

As she was tidying up the minimal mess from Charles's meal, Jacqui suddenly blurted out, "Charles, I would like you to get me off this godforsaken island. Do you think the ice is strong enough to support both of our weights on your snowmobile?"

Charles's jaw dropped and his eyebrows raised in amazement. "Are you quite sure, Mrs. Wilcox?" He needed to put some formality back into their interactions and insisted on using a more formal term of address. "I know the ice is strong enough, but do you really want to risk such a crossing? It would be safer in an airplane or helicopter, and I saw that there were several on the airstrip. I assume their pilots are still on the island, even though it is winter."

"Flying off the island has more risk for me… the risk of discovery. They would have to file flight plans along with a passenger manifest and I am too well-known on the island to fly under an alias," Jacqui explained. "You can see how much of an ogre my husband has become, and I cannot spend much more time as his captive here. You… have… to… help… me!" She buried her head in her hands and began sobbing, or so Charles thought; the sobs were merely theatrics intended to garner his sympathy.

"Jacqui," Charles began, using her given name for the first time, "I will help you get off the island, but we have only a couple of hours of daylight left and I would not want us to be caught out on the lake ice after dark. We should leave early tomorrow morning."

"Then you will have to spend the night. We have plenty of room," she said, "and the room will be at no cost to you. I imagine you will want a hot shower as well. The rooms are all *en suite*."

"A hot shower would be wonderful," Charles responded.

*   *   *   *   *

The next morning, with Charles Gordon Bruce devouring his breakfast in the kitchen, Jacqui delivered a tray upstairs to James. She had already eaten.

"James, here is your breakfast," she said without any feeling in her voice, "and… I would really appreciate it if you would take a shower soon. You stink. I could smell you as soon as I walked into the room."

James slammed his fist down onto the oak desktop and bellowed, "Dammit, woman! I'll take a shower when I'm damn good and ready. Can't you see I am working here?"

Jacqui was already nervous, preparing to run away for good. She had jumped noticeably when his fist boomed into the desktop. James's manifestation of anger was enough to convince her that she couldn't get off the island soon enough.

As she left James's office, she quietly closed the door and used an old skeleton key to lock it. Despite the age of the lock, it was still quite functional and did not make much noise when it engaged. James was so absorbed in his efforts that he didn't even notice.

"It serves him right. He deserves to be a prisoner in his own home," she thought as she pulled the key out of the keyhole, turned on her heel, and bounce-stepped down the corridor to the back staircase.

Seated in the kitchen and enjoying his second cup of coffee, Charles had heard most of the exchange taking place in James's office, which was directly overhead. The B&B was constructed in the late 19th Century and was far from soundproof. *"What am I getting myself into?"* he wondered, *"the last thing I need is to be caught in the middle of a nasty marital squabble."*

Jacqui returned to the kitchen, smiling as if nothing at all had happened upstairs. "It's time for us to go, Charles. I need a few minutes to put on my cold weather gear. The pantry is large enough that you can dress there if you like." The tone of her voice told him she meant business.

They were on their way less than a half an hour later and James Wilcox was none the wiser.

*   *   *   *   *

Around noon, James bellowed for Jacqui. "Woman, where's my lunch?" He was puzzled by the responding silence as Jacqui had always responded to his every beck and call. He bellowed again and received the same response: silence.

Now curious and wondering if something had befallen his wife elsewhere in the B&B, James rose from his desk and went to the door. Turning the crystal doorknob, he discovered that the door was locked from the outside. He was furious. "Jacqui, damn you! Come open this door immediately or I will break it down!"

Silence.

It took James about half an hour to break down the door with his body. In the months since Marcus's disappearance, James had let his body deteriorate and he was now so far out of shape that just a couple of body slams against the door left him breathless. He had to rest in between each attempt.

Once through the door, James huffed and puffed his way through the B&B trying to find Jacqui. She was nowhere to be found. Finally reaching the kitchen, he noticed dirty dishes in the sink, something totally out of character for his wife; in their decades of marriage, she had never left dishes sit in the sink for longer than a few minutes.

Turning around to the farmhouse dining table, he saw an envelope addressed to him in Jacqui's flowing script. His hands trembled as he opened the envelope and even more so as he unfolded the note. As he read, tears began to flow. His wife had left him. The reasons didn't matter.

"What have I done?" James asked himself as he slumped to the floor.

16: Our Own Paths
November – December 1813

Stephen Wilcox's revelation to me seemed irrational on the surface. *"Why would anyone want to remain here?"* I asked myself as I contemplated my own path forward. Forward to the 21st Century, that is.

I hypothesized that, since I had jumped backwards in time, there should also be a portal to the future. It seemed only logical that I would be able to make a reciprocal jump by reconstructing the same (or similar) situation that led to my appearance in 1813. But… I also faced the risk of going *back* in time another 204 years. That would have put me in the same year as the "Starving Time" at Jamestown, then one of only a couple of English settlements in the New World. Was I willing to take that risk, to travel back to a time even more primitive than 1813?

Stephen Wilcox had become besotted with Nurse Lizzie Pritchard, just as Simon Smithwick was with Nurse Christina Shelton. The looks they shared, the furtive touches I observed all pointed to much more than just casual friendships or work relationships. In my time, workplace romances were certainly frowned upon. Here, it was a different story. No one looked askance if two close work associates fell in love. In fact, it seemed to be encouraged in the absence of a pool of potentially suitable mates.

A few weeks after their return from their Chatham expedition, Doctor Wilcox and Nurse Pritchard presented themselves to me, both as nervous as long-tailed cats in a room full of rocking chairs. There seemed to be an aura of energy surrounding them and I immediately sensed what was to come next.

"Lieutenant Harris," Wilcox began, using the formalities of military address, "Nurse Pritchard and I would like… we are requesting your permission to be married as soon as possible."

"As soon as possible?" I queried.

"Yes, as soon as possible," Nurse Pritchard answered.

My mind was running amok. Was I about to lose half of my medical staff? Was the good nurse, usually a pantheon of virtue… pregnant? I had to know. My military training in my own time had taught me that personnel matters were best confronted directly, so I decided to apply that training to the present situation.

Tenting my fingers under my chin, I looked to the nurse. "Nurse Pritchard, are you… with child?"

"No, sir. I am not. Doctor Wilcox and I have remained chaste though presented with many opportunities to the contrary," she explained. "It is against my religion to… know… a man in the Biblical sense before we are husband and wife."

I was amazed by her openness, something that just did not happen in the early 19th Century. Women did not discuss such matters candidly with men other than their husbands or doctors; why was Nurse Pritchard being so forthcoming?

"Lieutenant, I hope that you will accede to our request forthwith," Wilcox interjected.

"I cannot afford to lose half of my medical staff. Will you stay here at Fort Malden after you are wed?" I asked, hopefully with enough urgency in my voice that they would understand my dilemma.

Wilcox responded, "Of course we will. We feel it is our duty to remain here caring for the wounded soldiers and any civilians from the surrounding area."

"Well, it's settled, then. You have my permission and will be afforded accommodations suitable for married people."

"Thank you, Marcus," Wilcox said, marking the end of the formal part of our conversation.

"Stephen, Lizzie… let me be the first to congratulate you on your impending nuptials. Would you like the Fort's chaplain to perform the ceremony?"

"He's Lutheran and we're both Roman Catholics. We will seek out the nearest priest to solemnize our vows in a formal Nuptial Mass. I have heard that there is an English-speaking priest across the river in Detroit," said Wilcox. "We wish to be married in the spring, after the thaw."

"Of course. I understand how important it is to keep to your own traditions," I agreed.

"Seaman Hardesty! Come here at once and bring a flask of rum with three mugs." Hardesty was my orderly and was always within earshot. He appeared a moment later, rum and mugs in hand. I took them from him and poured a liberal ration into each.

"I'd like to toast the future Doctor and Mrs. Stephen Wilcox!"

Barely an hour later, I would repeat the same scene as Doctor Smithwick and Nurse Shelton presented themselves to me, asking my permission for their own wedding. As with the previous couple, I queried if there was a child on the way; they gave me an almost identical answer to what Stephen and

Lizzie had given me. I was quickly becoming the odd man out.

I was nearer to forty than twenty and had never seriously considered matrimony as a way of life. The demands of my chosen profession, Explosive Ordnance Disposal, kept me in harm's way for most of my naval career. There was never an opportunity (nor did I have the desire) to settle down with a woman. My present situation didn't bode well for presenting any immediate opportunities, either. Wilcox and Smithwick had already emptied that pond.

17: Strange Encounters
January – February 1814

As the numbing cold wore on, we did indeed have to use the winter latrines on both sides of the river as Doctor Wilcox had suggested. The St. Clair River thankfully froze so solidly that it was possible to cross the ice with fully loaded wagons as needed. Out of an abundance of caution, however, I directed that the wagons be loaded only to half capacity.

By mid-February, our provisions were running low, thanks to spoilage of about half of our cured meat and fish. This situation forced me to order everyone to half rations, something I had hoped to avoid when first presented with the status of our stores.

Smithwick suggested that there might be a potentially friendly Potawatomi band on the Michigan side of the river, one that had remained neutral in the previous battles between the Americans and British. I decided that I should reach out to their elders in hopes of acquiring additional provisions. It was a huge gamble. Normally, the natives were very good hunters throughout the winter and likely would have quantities of cured meats set aside to help them survive the harsh conditions.

Smithwick knew the Potawatomi chief by name; translated, it meant "Shining Star." I was told that Shining Star also spoke fluent English and that he preferred to be addressed by the English translation because, as he put it, "the English sounds so much better than white men mispronouncing our language."

"Doctor Smithwick, do you think you could ride into the Potawatomi camp and set up a meeting?" I asked during our weekly status meeting.

"Yes, Lieutenant Harris. I will ride out to their village this afternoon and meet with Shining Star," he answered.

"Very well," I acknowledged.

*   *   *   *   *

Smithwick returned just before sunset. He was grinning from ear to ear. I could tell just from looking at him that the meeting with Shining Star had been a success.

Smithwick reported, "Lieutenant Harris, Shining Star will agree to help us with our predicament on one condition: that you meet with him personally. He told me that he will only make a deal with a man of similar standing, a chief. You are that chief. He expects to see you tomorrow morning."

Smithwick continued, "It is my recommendation that you not take an armed escort with you as a show of good faith. We have not engaged in any hostilities with this band and I do not think it would be wise to provoke them now that there are no longer any active or imminent military encounters in the area."

"Thank you, Doctor Smithwick. Your efforts in this matter are appreciated," I acknowledged.

Taking Smithwick at his word, I decided to assemble an entourage of uniformed but unarmed soldiers, including some of the walking wounded. It was a short distance west and south, to an area of the Michigan Territory with which I was intimately familiar, albeit in the 20th and 21st Centuries.

As we approached Shining Star's lodge, a young woman came out to greet us. Her jet-black hair glistened in the sun. Her eyes were dark as coal. Her face was... well... absolutely perfect. I could also see that, despite her winter attire, she was shapely in a healthy way and not an undernourished waif like the expectations of my own time.

"Do you speak English?" I asked as she came close enough to address in a normal speaking voice.

"Of course, I do, good sir. The Jesuit missionaries taught our entire village how to speak your language and French as well. We have been comfortable in either tongue for many summers," she answered.

"What is your name?" I asked.

"I am called 'White Moon' in your language," she answered.

"It is my pleasure to make your acquaintance, White Moon. My name is Marcus. Marcus Harris."

"Likewise, a pleasure, Mister Harris," she responded. Her eyes beamed as she tried to stifle a grin.

White Moon was absolutely gorgeous, and I was completely distracted by her beauty. With her presence, I would have agreed to almost any terms Shining Star proposed, even if they left us at a disadvantage.

White Moon swept the elk hide aside to admit us to Shining Star's lodge. I walked in and bowed low. "Shining Star, I am Lieutenant Marcus Harris of the United States Navy."

"Welcome, Lieutenant Harris. Your emissary, Doctor Smithwick, explained to me that you were in need of assistance. Can you assure me that nothing will be wasted if we reach an agreement here today?" Shining Star was all business. I sensed that he had been in this situation before and was thoroughly impressed by his command of *polite* English. It was music to my ears after months of listening to the expletives, epithets, and coarse pronunciations of the sailors and soldiers stuck at Fort Malden because of their injuries.

As if on cue, White Moon stood next to Shining Star. I was puzzled. Was she perhaps his wife?

"Lieutenant, I see you have already met my oldest daughter, White Moon. She has seen twenty-one summers and is without a husband."

Why would he be telling me this? What was he insinuating? Did he realize that I was two decades her senior and old enough to be her father myself?

The women of the camp served a wonderful mid-day meal consisting of root vegetables, fresh venison, turkey, and salt-cured fish. Everything was cooked or cured to perfection, far better than what the camp cooks produced every day. My assigned seat was nearest Shining Star, one that was normally reserved for esteemed guests and elders White Moon had been given the responsibility of personally tending to my needs as we ate; her smile was electric and could have lit up a darkened room.

"Harris, get ahold of yourself! You're not that kind of man!" I admonished myself. Internal arguments aside, I was smitten. I had to know more about White Moon.

The meal concluded, I could now get down to business with Shining Star. It was Fort Malden that needed something from the Potawatomi, so I had to be polite and deferential in my negotiations. One misstep or *faux pas* on my part could put a stop to any deal between us.

I explained our situation to Shining Star in detail, focusing on our lack of food and the condition of our wounded soldiers. With winter isolating us from our forces, there was little or no chance of resupply or evacuation, Without Shining Star's help, our survival until spring would be in jeopardy. I did not want to be put in a position to decide who got fed and who didn't.

"Lieutenant Harris," Shining Star intoned, "we agree that you have fallen on hard times and need food for your men at the fort. I will provide a whole deer every week, perhaps more, for you to feed your men. All I ask is that it not be wasted."

"Yes, of course," I agreed.

"To make sure that you do not waste any of Mother Earth's gifts, I will send my daughter, White Moon, back to Fort Malden with you. She will instruct your cooks how to use every bit of the deer." Shining Star's tone was as if he were giving a royal decree; his word had the force of law in this area and everyone in his village knew it.

"Thank you, Shining Star. You have been most gracious," I acknowledged.

"It is better for us to help you with food than it is to take care of the bodies of your dead," he replied. "It would be a shame for us to have to bury all of you because you starved to death."

Shining Star was a better diplomat than any Foreign Service Officer I had encountered in my military career. He had grasped the situation, made a decision that was consistent with the needs of all concerned, and then provided an implementation plan. *And my ancestors called these people savages,* I thought to myself. Nothing could have been further from the truth.

*　*　*　*　*

As the coldest days and nights passed, White Moon proved that she was indeed the daughter of a tribal elder. Her regal bearing and assertion of authority amazed me. I had

131

never in all my years seen a woman who could establish command as quickly as she had. She also began attending my status meetings and kept us apprised of our food stores. She was a master logistician, something that neither I nor my two doctors ever seemed to master. On more than one occasion, we ran out of bandages before I was informed of the situation.

When we were not engaged in the business of Fort Malden, White Moon and I spent quite a bit of time together. She began teaching me some of her customs and language; I was a willing pupil, taking in everything she was teaching. The ways of her family and village fascinated me, especially with regard to marriage and child-rearing.

After a meal in the galley with the two doctors and their now-affianced nurses aboard the *Lawrence*, White Moon walked with me back to my quarters. It was a cold, clear night and the stars shone. To the north, ribbons of the *aurora borealis* shimmered in hues of red, green, blue, and gold. It was an almost magical setting.

Reaching the door of my cabin, I was shocked as White Moon took my hand in hers. It was a tender touch that sent shivers up my arm and through my body, something that I had never felt before. *"What is happening here?"* I wondered.

I didn't have to wait long to find out. With subtle pressure, she pulled me close, close enough that I could feel the heat of her breath on my chest. I was even more surprised when she addressed me by my given name, not my rank.

Looking up into my eyes, she said, "Marcus, you may kiss me if you wish."

"White Moon, I would like nothing better than to kiss you right now," I replied.

For the next several minutes, we remained coupled in a passionate embrace, sharing tender kisses in the cold darkness, a cold which neither of us felt despite our lack of appropriate cold weather clothing. We were oblivious to our surroundings and focused only on each other.

It might have been only minutes; it could just as easily have been hours. I had very little experience in the physical aspects of a male-female relationship; sure, I had sowed my wild oats in my late teens and early during my Navy career before I was placed into leadership positions, but this was something completely different. Powerful. Consuming. Soul-reaching. I was smitten.

White Moon usually returned to her assigned berth with the two nurses. Tonight, however, she did not. After the change of watch around midnight, I unlocked the door to my cabin and beckoned her to join me inside. She followed willingly and without hesitation.

18: New Beginnings
March 1814

The assistance from Shining Star's hunters and White Moon's leadership were making a difference in our ability to survive the harsh winter conditions. I no longer feared widespread starvation nor disease brought on by too many bodies confined in too small a space to conserve heat. We would survive.

Surviving, too, was my relationship with White Moon. Since our first tryst late that cold February night, we had shared my bed repeatedly and she now believed she was with child. In the custom of her people, it was appropriate for her to declare us married and for me to claim the child as my own. However, both would require permission from her grandmother, She-Eagle, the matriarch of the village.

"White Moon, are you certain you wish to take this white man as your husband?" She-Eagle asked when we declared our intentions. Her tone was stern but playful.

"Yes, Grandmother She-Eagle. I do not wish to lie with any other man," White Moon replied.

The next question surprised me. It was usually women's business and whispered over the cooking fires.

"White Moon, how long has it been since you last bled?" She-Eagle asked, looking directly into White Moon's coal-black eyes.

"Three moons have passed, Grandmother She-Eagle," White Moon replied. "I expect to be a mother around the time of the harvest."

She-Eagle nodded before turning to me, "Lieutenant Harris, do you accept the child White Moon carries as your own?" I was shocked that She-Eagle still would not address me by my given name, instead choosing formality for this situation.

"Yes, Grandmother She-Eagle. I do." I was trembling as I responded. I was going to have a wife and become a father, neither of which I was really prepared for.

My mind wandered, even as I spoke to She-Eagle and White Moon. This new situation complicated any efforts to return to my own time, 204 years into the future. Unless I could take White Moon and our child with me, I would be obliged to remain here in 1814. I then remembered how Doctor Wilcox had also jumped across time from 1992. Was he wondering the same things that I was, albeit minus the encumbrance of a baby? I had to find out.

"White Moon, Marcus…" She-Eagle spoke, using my given name for the first time, perhaps indicating that I was now part of their extended family, "you are married in the eyes of this village. May you be blessed by the Earth Mother with many more children and be happy together into old age."

Turning to me, She-Eagle added one more statement confirming what I had already assessed, "Marcus Harris, you are now one of us. We welcome you." She leaned forward and kissed me lightly on each cheek, a custom I assumed was of French origin but would later learn was Potawatomi, having existed long before French explorers or Jesuit missionaries ever visited the area.

I was surprised to learn that we were now entitled to our own private lodge in their village, based on White Moon's status as daughter of the ruling family. The lodge was close enough to the river crossing that we could spend some of our time there instead of on board the *Lawrence*. It was in this lodge that we spent our wedding night.

*   *   *   *   *

Back aboard the *Lawrence* two days later, I convened a meeting of my staff: Doctors Wilcox and Smithwick; Nurses

Pritchard and Shelton; my orderly, Seaman Hardesty; and, my *wife*, White Moon.

Calling the meeting to order, my voice wavered as I spoke. "Ladies and Gentlemen, first and foremost, I have an announcement to make. White Moon and I are now husband and wife. She is with child and expects to be delivered of a baby around harvest time in the fall."

Congratulations resounded from my team. Even the normally taciturn Doctor Smithwick was effusive with his praise. Wilcox, though at first congratulatory, took me aside for a private moment.

"Marcus, are you sure of what you are doing, marrying a… much younger woman?" he asked. I was sure he was more concerned that she was Potawatomi than he was about her age.

"I've been without a wife long enough," I countered, "and White Moon is everything I could want in a woman. And, if you must know, *she* chose *me* – not the other way around, like we do. It is her people's custom for the woman to choose their own husband. It helped that I was already in love with her."

"Dude, you've never been this open about your feelings in your life at least not to another man," I told myself silently.

Wilcox just shook his head. He was not buying any of what I was telling him. He had always been cordial to White Moon, but there was always a disdainful tone to his voice, as if she wasn't good enough for him to be talking to. I could not let it fester and impact on the relationships within our staff or the Potawatomi village. White Moon was my wife, part of my staff, and our liaison with the village; Wilcox would just have to get over it.

I would soon learn that White Moon, too, had sensed Wilcox's veiled condescension.

A few nights later, while we were away from the *Lawrence* and in our lodge in the Native village, White Moon shared her concerns with me.

"Marcus, Doctor Wilcox doesn't seem to like me very much," White Moon began.

"I've noticed it, too," I answered. "Once we get to the spring thaw and the last of the wounded are discharged, I will release Doctor Wilcox from his obligation. The United States is now in control of this entire region and rejoining the fight elsewhere would be far too difficult."

I knew that most of the action was at least a week away on horseback – and being in the wilderness, we were far removed from regular messenger communications. It had been weeks since we had last seen a courier and even longer since I was able to pay the men with any more than scrip guaranteeing conversion to cash as soon as it was available.

Now, as a married man and potential father, I also had more pressing matters to deal with than the likes of Doctor Wilcox.

"White Moon, I do not want our child to be separated from the ways of your people. He or she should know both of our customs," I said softly as I nuzzled against her neck.

"Marcus, I would not have it any other way," she cooed. "Can you see yourself remaining here in Michigan Territory once the war is over?"

"That all depends on you, my dear. Remember, *you* chose *me!*"

She giggled playfully before kissing me tenderly and guiding my hand to her breast.

*   *   *   *   *

A week went by before I convened another staff meeting. It was time to confront Doctor Wilcox. I could not put it off any longer as his attitude had gotten progressively worse by the day.

At the end of the meeting, I dismissed everyone except Wilcox. He stood in front of my worktable with a puzzled look on his face. To maintain an element of formality, I had to speak first.

"Doctor Wilcox," I began, using the most serious tone I could muster, "I sense that you do not like the fact that I have married a Potawatomi woman. The tone of your voice when you speak to or about her tells me that you hold irrational animosity towards our native friends. Do you care to explain yourself?"

"Marcus –"

I interrupted him before he could continue. "Please, Doctor, this is a formal situation, and I must ask that you respect the decorum of the moment," I said in my best no-nonsense tone. He knew that I was expecting him to address me by my rank, devoid of familiarity.

"Of course, Lieutenant Harris. As you wish," he replied.

"We must find a way to get you back to 1992," I explained. "Your attitude of late is having a detrimental impact on the staff and could potentially endanger our fragile relationship with the Potawatomi. I hope we can find a time portal before the spring thaw, as I will have no other choice than to release you from your obligation to the United States at that time."

"As you wish, Lieutenant," he acknowledged.

"It might be worth sending you back to New Haven, where your time travel began, but that would take several weeks and be fraught with danger as you would be traveling on your own, with no military escort."

"If it comes to that," Wilcox answered, "I will take that risk."

"Will you be leaving Nurse Pritchard behind if you are able to jump back to the 20th Century, to 1994?" I asked.

"Absolutely not. Lizzie needs to come with me. We cannot be apart from each other once we are married," Wilcox said sternly.

I thought for a couple of moments before responding. In the silence, I could see that Wilcox was getting nervous. He wanted Nurse Pritchard to come with him, but he was unsure of both the possibility of her traveling across time with him and whether she would fit in. I was also wondering if he had even attempted to explain to her that he was from the future.

I finally broke the silence and returned to a less formal tone. "Stephen, you mentioned that something like Hecate's Wheel was responsible for your jumping backwards in time. White Moon showed me a glyph carved into the bark of a tree in the forest a few miles west of her village. It was an embellished circle that she said represented a gateway of some kind, and she thought it was linked to fertility and motherhood. She did say it was from the "old ways" and not part of their blended Christian customs. Do you think you could draw what you saw in the church crypt in New Haven? I think there might be a connection."

"Marcus, the symbol in the crypt is burned into my memory. Do you have paper and a quill? It won't take me long to draw what I remember."

I watched as Stephen painstakingly drew the Wheel he had touched in the New Haven church. After seeing his case books, I knew that his drawing would be very precise. He started with a simple circle, then drew an elaborate maze within that circle. It was nearly identical to the tree carving White Moon had shown me in one of our woodland trysts. I could hardly contain my excitement.

"Stephen! That is almost an exact duplicate of what White Moon showed me in the forest," I exclaimed. "It might be a time portal… I think I could find it again, but I don't want to risk offending White Moon's family if I take you there without a Potawatomi escort. It could have some sacred significance to the older members of the tribe."

19: Into the Woods
Early April, 1814

For our first foray into the woods to find the Wheel that White Moon had shown me, the party consisted of myself, White Moon, Doctor Wilcox, Nurse Pritchard, and our Potawatomi guide, White Moon's younger brother, *Seksi-pto*. Wilcox and I were both armed with pistols and knives. White Moon was the only woman who was armed; she carried her own heirloom skinning knife sheathed in the waistbelt of her buckskins. Her similarly dressed brother, *Seksi-pto,* was carrying a bow, quiver full of arrows, a tomahawk, a long knife, and a short dagger.

In their language, *Seksi-pto* meant 'running deer,' he explained in fluent English. It was the first real conversation we had attempted since I had married his sister in the Potawatomi way.

"May I call you 'Running Deer' instead of '*Seksi-pto*'?" I asked, trying to remain as deferent as possible to their culture. "It is much easier for me to pronounce."

"Yes, Marcus, that would be acceptable," Running Deer replied. I could see White Moon's beaming smile as I spoke to her brother. It was a watershed moment for my acceptance into her band. Despite Grandmother She-Eagle's edicts approving our marriage, acceptance by the rest of the band had been slow in coming.

As I spoke with Running Deer, I sensed Wilcox's growing anxiety. He wanted to find the glyph and attempt to jump forward to 1992. It didn't take long before he vocalized that impatience.

"Come on, Harris, can we please get on with this? I don't have time for you and your wife to make eyes at each other," Wilcox moaned.

"Would you please try to avoid offending my wife and her family any more than you already have?" I retorted. His petulance was starting to grate on my nerves, and I was more than ready to send him back to where he came from, 180 years in the future.

Lizzie Pritchard, dressed uncharacteristically in trousers and a man's hunting shirt, had remained silent through all of this, and I could see her uneasiness growing Her mood, however, was caused by her prospective husband and not by any of the events going on around her. *"Was she having second thoughts?"* I wondered to myself.

"Doctor Wilcox, a word if I may?" I had to find out what, if anything, he had told Nurse Pritchard.

"Yes, of course, Lieutenant," he replied.

We stepped away from the rest of the group and out of earshot. I did not want them to overhear what we were discussing.

"Stephen, have you told Lizzie about where… when… you came from?" I asked.

"As a matter of fact, I have not," he replied. "I thought it would be easier for her to just make the jump to 1994 with me without an elaborate explanation. I was planning to explain everything to her once we had crossed the time boundary."

Wilcox paused for a moment, then continued, "Besides, we aren't entirely sure that she will be able to accompany me anyway. If she is left here in 1814, it's no big deal. If she disintegrates in the transit, well… I probably won't even know, except that she won't have arrived with me. Any way you look at it, Stephen, it is best that I not try to explain it all to her. At least not now."

Now he was making sense.

My thoughts did wander to an earlier conversation where he swore that he had found his niche here in 1814. He was also emphatic about not really needing a wife. I guess love will do that to a man, as I had discovered first-hand.

We returned to the rest of our little group about half an hour later. Darkness was almost upon us, and I wondered if we should make camp and wait until morning before sending Stephen and Lizzie on their way. My pensive mood was not lost on my wife, White Moon.

"Marcus, I know why you brought us here," she said calmly. "The circle maze on the tree is an opening in time. It has been a legend of our people for many, many years – since before the first missionaries converted us to Christianity. We don't know where it leads or what is on the other side, as none of my people have ever returned after passing through it."

She continued, "And now, Doctor Wilcox wants to go back to his own time. Is he from the future, or from the past?"

"White Moon, before I answer you about Doctor Wilcox's origin, I have to ask you a question,"

"Yes, my husband?"

"Would you be surprised to know that I am also from another place in time?"

White Moon thought for a few moments before she answered, "I knew from when I first met you that you were different. I did not know exactly why I felt that way, but now that you have told me, it all makes sense."

Something in her eyes and the way she was rubbing her… still very small baby bump… told me I still had a lot of explaining to do. The first thing I needed to do was to reassure her that I was not planning to go back to 2017 unless I was sure that both she and the baby would make the journey with me. Wilcox, as I had discovered in our conversation, didn't care one bit about what happened to Lizzie Pritchard. He was only concerned about himself.

"White Moon, Grandmother She-Eagle has already welcomed me to the lodges of the Keepers of the Fire, your people… I do not wish to offend any of you."

I suddenly realized I had just made a blunder of epic proportions: I had forgotten White Moon and our growing baby. They were certainly more important than her grandmother and the rest of the tribe. I needed to fix my mistake, and fast.

I looked into her deep brown, almost black, eyes, and crooned softly, "White Moon, I could never leave you nor our baby. If I go, you go. I will not even attempt to go back to my time unless I am absolutely certain you will be there by my side with our child. All you have to do is ask me to stay here and I will."

The Potawatomi were known for being quite unemotional and stoic when they were unhappy or faced with a difficult situation. Despite her upbringing, White Moon's expression suddenly changed. Tears welled up in her eyes and flowed freely down her cheeks.

"Marcus… my husband… I will love you to the ends of the earth. I am honored for you to call me your wife. I know you mean every word you say and that you will never leave us behind – unlike that *shegak*… skunk, Stephen Wilcox. He doesn't care one bit for Lizzie's feelings, and I think that is why he convinced her to wait until the spring thaw to be married," she explained through the tears.

As I held her close, it dawned on me that her analysis of the situation couldn't be any more correct. Wilcox would not hesitate to leave Lizzie behind even after they were married. His only objective was to get back to his own time, 180 years in the future – no matter the personal cost.

I remembered my conversation with him a few days earlier when he described Hecate's Wheel to me. He started tracing the perimeter from the bottom, counterclockwise, and getting stuck at top dead center. *"I wonder if I can trick him into continuing the counterclockwise circle until he is back at the bottom again,"* I mused. *"That would send him back in time instead of forward, putting him in 1634 – when the area was still largely unknown to European explorers and missionaries."*

"Marcus," White Moon said as she regained her composure, "only the grandmothers, like She-Eagle, are allowed to know the full story. Someday, I will be a grandmother myself and will have the story handed down to me. Until then, I must simply accept whatever happens here with Doctor Wilcox and Lizzie."

"Do you think She-Eagle will allow me to know the secret?" I asked.

"Of that I am not sure," White Moon replied, "but you will not know until you ask her that question yourself."

"It may be too late to ask her. Wilcox seems determined to walk through the portal tonight," I said. "I have already recommended that we make camp for the night and send them on their way at sunrise tomorrow."

Returning to what would be our overnight camp, Running Deer had already started a fire and Lizzie was tending it, adding more wood to it as the kindling began to burn. Wilcox was nowhere in sight; after a few moments, I heard a gunshot and realized that he had probably gone hunting for our supper. A few minutes later, I heard a second shot.

Wilcox returned to our makeshift camp with two large fox squirrels in hand. They would be enough to provide the four of us with a decent meal, added to the Potawatomi equivalent of hardtack that we all carried in our belt pouches.

Conversation during our meal was sporadic at best and the tension was palpable. Wilcox and I knew what could lie ahead for him. Given that he had not informed Lizzie of his intentions to take her with him into the future, I did not feel it was my place to offer any commentary, so I spoke little. White Moon knew of his plans, too, but also recognized the situation as one where it was best to keep quiet; not even "women's talk" would have been appropriate.

An almost full moon rose over the woods and bathed our camp in a silvery glow. The moonlight also illuminated the carving of Hecate's Wheel in a ghostly, spectral light. The exposed hardwood of the very large oak tree literally glowed. The eerie vision sent a chill down my spine and made goosebumps rise on my forearms.

After a while, Wilcox and I were alone in the camp. Running Deer, armed with a knife, a tomahawk and his bow and quiver, had accompanied the two women into the woods to take care of bodily functions. It was necessary for the women to have an armed escort as the area was known for bears, wolves, and bobcats. Their absence gave me another chance to speak with Stephen Wilcox.

"Stephen, I strongly suggest that you do whatever it is you plan on doing while it is still dark," I said in a near-whisper.

"I agree, Marcus," Wilcox replied. "We will be on our way as soon as the women return." That said, he turned towards the fire as an indication that he had nothing further to say.

It was with only minor trepidation that I accepted Wilcox's desire for a quick departure. I knew he was unhappy here in 1814 and that going to another time was in his best interests. But should I be vindictive and try to send him *backward* in time instead of forward to his origin? Every indication was there that movement forward or backward in time was a function of the finger trace direction around the circumference of the circle.

Running Deer, White Moon and Lizzie Pritchard returned from their foray into the woods. They were in good spirits, and Lizzie was a lot less sullen and detached than she was when they left. In fact, the two ladies were giggling like schoolgirls sharing a private joke. Running Deer, on the other hand, simply shrugged his shoulders. He was a man and not subject to such frivolity. I wondered just how long the ladies' levity would last.

20: Will the Circle Be Broken?
Still Early April, 1814

Running Deer, as our guide, was responsible for our overall safety in the woods. Once he brought the women back to our camp, he left once more to do what we in the military would have called a perimeter reconnaissance. Ranging out from our camp approximately one hundred yards, he made sure that there were no potential bandits nearby, that there was no threatening wildlife like bears or wolves, and that we would be able to hear anyone or anything approaching in the darkness. Running Deer moved so quietly that his movements were undetectable even to my combat-trained ears.

While Running Deer was away and before the women could begin setting out their bedrolls for the night, Wilcox stood and took Lizzie's hand.

"Come with me, Lizzie… This circle carved into the tree is supposed to be filled with good luck," he explained. "If we trace the circle together, our union will be happy and blessed."

"What a load of baloney," I thought to myself, *"he still hasn't told her about the possibility of their time travel."*

White Moon raised an eyebrow and looked at me with her own expression of disbelief, as if she was reading my mind. She knew how full of nonsense Wilcox's statements really were. He was only concerned with his own departure for another time; whether Lizzie was able to go with him remained immaterial and inconvenient.

Lizzie trembled as they approached the Hecate's Wheel carving. Wilcox had his hand clasped around hers; she would be the first one to touch-trace the circle. The circle still glowed in the moonlight, as if it were calling for someone to touch it. The high cirrus clouds seemed to make the intensity of the light pulse as the moonlight faded in and out.

For a moment, they stood motionless and silent at the base of the tree. With his right hand, Wilcox guided Lizzie's left hand to the top of the circle and firmly pressed her index finger to the top of the circumference. As she touched the circle, we felt a vibration like a low magnitude earthquake beneath our feet. Wilcox guided Lizzie's hand counterclockwise around the circle as the vibrations intensified.

"Counterclockwise! Yes!" I nearly blurted out. If my hypothesis was correct, Wilcox and/or Lizzie would be going backward in time.

Slowly, the trace continued to the left, toward the bottom of the circle, with Lizzie's fingertip remaining in constant contact; Stephen Wilcox's hand covered hers but was not touching the carving himself.

"Was he up to something?" I wondered. *"He's not touching the glyph, just Lizzie."*

After what seemed like an eternity frozen in time, there was a blinding series of strobe-like flashes and loud clap of what we all would later think was thunder. White Moon had been standing next to me but was now nowhere to be seen. The same for Stephen Wilcox and Lizzie Pritchard. Both were gone. The only thing still intact from the few minutes before the flash-bang was the glyph carved into the tree – and its eerie glow had increased ten-fold. Running Deer, or so I thought, had been away from the camp on his patrol and I imagined that he had not been affected by what had just transpired.

I then realized there was a steady ringing in my ears, worse than what I had ever experienced from firing weapons when I was in the Navy. I called for White Moon and heard only the echo of my own voice. I hoped the near deafness would only be temporary.

Realizing that I was unable to move anything other than my arms, shoulders, neck, and head, my Navy training kicked in: I did a rapid self-assessment and determined that I was neither bleeding nor seriously injured. Concerned that I had suffered a spinal injury paralyzing my lower extremities, I grabbed a pointed stick that was within an arm's reach and poked in firmly into my thigh, just above my kneecap. "Ouch!" I exclaimed in a loud whisper, repeating the test on my other leg with the same result. Thankfully, I still had pain sensations; that was one of the field tests we were taught to evaluate the severity of wounds sustained by our comrades-in-arms.

As the ringing in my ears subsided, I hoped that my companions (perhaps except for Stephen Wilcox) had not sustained any significant injuries, either. Confirmation of that was quick in coming.

"Marcus? Are you there?" It was White Moon!

"I am here, my darling. Are you hurt?" I asked. The sound of her lilting voice was music to my ears.

"I appear to be unable to move my legs," she replied.

"It will pass. I was the same way a few minutes ago and can now move my toes." I said as calmly as I could.

'Do you know where *Seksi-pto*... Running Deer... is?" she asked.

"I am here, sister." It was Running Deer. His voice sounded full of life and authority. "Thank God and Mother Earth that you were spared," he said reverently. "What just happened here? I saw the flashes of lightning and heard the sound of thunder, but no storm clouds in the sky." Apparently, he had returned to our camp unnoticed just as Lizzie, under duress from Wilcox, was tracing the circle with her finger.

Now almost fully in control of my legs, I stood unsteadily and surveyed our surroundings. The undergrowth up to twenty yards out from the base of the tree had been flattened by some undetermined kinetic force. Just outside that circle, from diametrically opposed locations, I could see both White Moon and Running Deer slowly coming upright to seated positions.

There was still no sign of Stephen Wilcox nor Lizzie Pritchard. Did they make the jump in time? I decided to start a grid search using the glyph tree as my datum point and briefly explained to Running Deer what I was about to do. He understood immediately.

"Just like tracking a wounded animal," he grinned. The irony of his statement was not lost on me.

After about half an hour of searching, we found Stephen Wilcox. Propped up against a tree as if he had sat there intentionally, he was in a catatonic state and totally unresponsive to our verbal entreaties regarding his condition. The only movement was the occasional blinking of his eyes, but that movement was not in response to anything we were saying.

While Running Deer continued the grid search in hopes of finding Lizzie Pritchard, my buddy-care training kicked in. I had to assess Wilcox's condition if we were to even consider moving him from where he sat. He could have a spinal injury – or worse.

Once again using my pointy stick, I prodded the upturned palm of Wilcox's right hand. He clenched it into a fist and quickly withdrew it from the cause of the pain. That ruled out any injury to his upper spine.

Next, I did the same pain test on his left leg, poking the point into the flesh just above his ankle bone. Again, he jumped in response. No apparent nerve damage to his lower back, either.

There was no explanation for his catatonia other than proximity to the glyph and Lizzie Pritchard at the time of the… whatever it was we had just experienced. We had to revive him if we were to determine what happened in the flash-bang moment. Other than the pain tests, nothing I attempted was having any effect.

I had seen similar responses to firefights in combat zones in my previous – upcoming – life. After a hostile engagement, some participants simply withdrew into themselves. Our unit psychologists always recommended that, assuming the location was safe, we let the affected warrior rest as long as necessary before attempting movement. The shrinks explained that the post-stress catatonia usually resolved once the cortisol levels of a fight-or-flight response subsided sufficiently.

Wilcox's "recovery" from his catatonia was quite sudden and dramatic. He blinked his eyes several times, shook his head from side to side, and then uttered, "Where am I?"

When he saw me standing there, he screwed his face into a puzzled scowl. "Marcus, if you are here, you either made the jump with me or I'm stuck in 1814. Please tell me which is true."

"Stephen, we aren't exactly sure ourselves," I explained, "there was a blinding flash, what sounded like a clap of thunder, and then nothing. I think we were all unconscious for several minutes."

"Where's Lizzie?" he asked. Wilcox was on the verge of panic in spite of his earlier indifference. "Lizzie? Are you here?" "Lizzie?" "Where are you?"

"Stephen, please try to remain calm. Running Deer is still with us and is searching the area for Lizzie as we speak. White Moon is still here, too. Running Deer should be back soon."

Running Deer had silently returned to the perimeter of our camp, avoiding Wilcox's line of sight. He did, however, give me a quick nod that I understood to mean that he wanted to speak with me privately.

"Stephen, stay here. I will be right back," I told him before crossing the small clearing to speak with Running Deer.

"Marcus," Running Deer whispered, "you must come with me. What I found is quite disturbing." I nodded my assent as he blended back into the moonlit foliage and invisibility as I returned to Stephen Wilcox.

"Stephen, you must watch over White Moon for a few moments while I go out to take care of... well... you know..." It was the best excuse I could think of to get me out of the camp for a few minutes to rendezvous with Running Deer.

"Marcus, come with me, please. It isn't far," Running Deer whispered.

After maybe fifty yards into the woods away from camp, he pointed down at the ground. I was speechless when I observed a messy pile of clothing, shoes, and a woman's undergarments. I looked at the clothing: it was the same trousers and hunting shirt Lizzie had been wearing before the flash-bang moment. I deduced that she must have made the jump – to a time when her clothes, and especially the trousers, would not have been appropriate.

Lizzie Pritchard must have jumped backward in time. Trousers for women, and even hunting shirts, were appropriate dress for 1994, which was 180 years into the future from 1814. The other direction, to 1634, was more likely as European women of that time *never* wore trousers. I remembered from my earlier discussions with Stephen Wilcox how he found himself naked in the woods after jumping back from 1992, which we deduced was the result of inappropriate clothing for the period.

Now that we had more or less confirmed that Lizzie Pritchard was no longer on our timeline, we had to establish *when* we were. The campsite and moon phase were the same as they were before the flash-bang. The foliage, what little there was of it, was appropriate for the first week in April. The only way we would know for sure would be to return to Detroit, Fort Malden, or the *Lawrence*.

"I think we should gather up Lizzie's clothing and take them back to Stephen as evidence of her departure," I explained to Running Deer.

"Agreed," he replied, and took it upon himself to pick up her clothing and respectfully tie it into a bundle. He chanted softly as he worked; its timing and context told me it was a haunting chant for one who had crossed over to the spirit world. *"This band of Potawatomi may have converted to Christianity,"* I told myself, *"but they still clung to some of their old ways, especially where death is concerned."*

When we returned to our camp, Stephen and White Moon were chatting amiably next to the fire. It was as if they were long-lost best friends. The amiability, however, would be short-lived.

With our heads bowed, Running Deer and I approached Stephen.

"Doctor Wilcox," I began, choosing formality over familiarity, "we have some upsetting news."

"Yes? Go on," he said with a wave of his hand. "Tell me what you have to tell me."

"It appears that Lizzie has disappeared," I explained. "We found her clothing in a wrinkled pile not far from the tree carving. Do you remember your own experience? Clothing from the 1990s would not have been appropriate here – and Lizzie's trousers and hunting shirt certainly wouldn't have been appropriate in 1634, which is where I believe she has gone. She may be lying naked in this very clearing right now, but 180 years in our past."

Wilcox let out a primal scream so loud that any nearby wildlife would have been frightened away. It resonated through the woods like no other sound I had ever heard.

White Moon cradled Stephen Wilcox in her arms as he wept hysterically. She seemed puzzled by his behavior as it was probably the first time she had ever been exposed to an emotional and tearful outburst from a man.

Through his sobs, I could hear phrases like *"I did it to her..."* or *"What have I done?"* He was filled with remorse. He had forced Lizzie's hand around the circle. It should have been him that had disappeared, presumably back 180 years, to 1634.

21: Lizzie
Potawatomi Territory, April 1634

In 1634, the area that would become part of the Michigan Territory in 1805 and the State of Michigan in 1838 was still a wilderness. The first French explorers and Catholic missionaries are believed to have transited the area in the 1620s under the auspices of Samuel de Champlain as Governor of New France. However, permanent European settlements in the area were still several years in the future.

*   *   *   *   *

Lizzie Pritchard regained consciousness thinking she was still near Stephen Wilcox, Marcus Harris, White Moon, and Running Deer. Suddenly very cold, she realized she was completely naked. There was no campfire. There were no other people. The ornate circle carving in the tree was the only thing that had any connection to where she had just been. *"Am I having a bad dream?"* she wondered to herself.

Rolling over onto her stomach and rising to a kneeling position, she vomited violently into the underbrush next to her. When the vomiting subsided into dry heaves, she tried to stand and take stock of her surroundings. Where she was looked similar, but decidedly different, from what she remembered. The trees were younger – except for the carved tree – and smaller in circumference. The undergrowth was not as dense. There were no remnants of a recent campfire that she clearly remembered White Moon tending after cooking their delicious squirrel dinner.

Lizzie's disorientation and dehydration were taking their toll. She called out, "Help!" "Help!" "Help me, please!" but her voice was barely above a whisper.

A rustling in the bushes brought Lizzie close to panic. If it was an animal, she had no weapon with which to protect herself. If the sound was that of a human, she was indecently exposed. She finally decided that any animal making that much noise was probably a predator and could easily maul her to death, not caring if she was clothed or naked. In case it *was* a human, she used her hands to cover her breasts and pubic area and defend her modesty against prying human eyes.

What Lizzie had not yet realized was that she had been transformed from an attractive woman to a wizened old crone. Gone were her solid good looks; in their place were warts and wrinkles. She slumped forward from her shoulders and had become the epitome of witches common to children's fairy tales.

"Hello? Who's there?" she called again, the panic in her voice rising.

The nearly full moon provided quite a bit of light, but it was still not quite enough to see more than shadows or silhouettes. Looking in the direction of the noise, Lizzie clearly saw the outline of a human form. As she stared trying to focus her vision more clearly, she heard another noise immediately behind her. Whipping around and forgetting to keep her private regions covered, she saw another shape, but this time the shape was close enough she could clearly see human facial features. She would not be mauled to death by a predator after all!

As their eyes locked, both the intruder and Lizzie screamed. She, because she was truly frightened. He, because he had never seen a white woman before, and especially not a naked one that looked more like a forest dweller than a human being.

After a few tense moments, the man began calling loudly in a language she did not understand. She was conversant in French and had also studied German and Latin. The sound was nothing even close to those three languages.

"*Mendozet!*" "*Mendozet!*" "*Mendozet!*" (Witch!) the man screamed over and over again. "*Nem, Mendozet!*" (Go away, witch!). After repeating this several times, he added arm motions and pointing to clarify his intended meaning.

"Sir, I do not understand," Lizzie answered. "Do you speak English?" Silence.

She tried French. "*Parlez-vous Français?*" Nothing.

"*Sprechen Sie Deutsch?*" No German, either.

Finally, in desperation, she tried Latin. "*Loquerisne Anglice?*" The man remained deadpan.

The man, dressed in animal skins against the cold, stopped waving his arms and approached Lizzie. She froze and remained motionless as his hand reached out and touched her face, then her breasts, then her genitals. After this invasive examination he seemed convinced that she was a human being after all. Still, her appearance was puzzling: even the oldest woman in his village was not this ugly.

Looking across the clearing to his partner he said, "*Nabma. Myanze. Windgowi. Mendozet. Neshewet.*" Look at her. She is ugly. A monster. A witch. A murderer.

That was all the partner needed. He already had his flint knife in hand and, with a blood-curdling whoop, set upon Lizzie. In a matter of seconds, she was no longer among the living.

22: New Orders
Vicinity of Detroit and Fort Malden, April 1814

As we headed back to Detroit, Fort Malden, and the *Lawrence*, White Moon talked almost nonstop about her people's history. There apparently was a legend, handed down through the generations, of a female forest monster who was killed by a hunting party not far from where the glyph was carved into the tree.

"It was before the missionaries came," she said. "The legend said the monster seemed human but was not pretty to look at and made the strangest sounds."

I wondered if that legend was Lizzie Pritchard. Or perhaps it was another time traveler? We would never know.

Because we had been away from the field hospital for several days already, I felt it necessary to return and receive a report from Doctor Smithwick.

"Welcome back, Lieutenant Harris!" Smithwick said warmly.

"Has anything of importance happened since I was away?"

"No, sir. The men all seem to be healthy and are continuing their recoveries. We have not had a case of the bloody flux since before you left. By the end of the month, I expect that the wounded men will all be able to be released from care," Smithwick explained.

"Very well," I acknowledged.

"Lieutenant, there is one other thing…" Smithwick said almost sheepishly.

"What is it?" I asked.

"A courier arrived yesterday from General Harrison's headquarters. He is waiting in the visitor's tent for your return."

I wondered what might be in store for me. We had not had a dispatch from Harrison since before Christmas and had been left on our own with no new supplies. The harsh winter saw Lake Erie deeply frozen and deep snow had made travel for any considerable distance all but impossible. I was now certain that the courier I had sent in the other direction at the beginning of December never made it to Harrison, which explained our lack of replenishments.

As I walked through the open flap of the visitors' tent, the courier, a private, stood stiffly to attention and saluted.

"Sir! I have an urgent dispatch from General Harrison and Commodore Perry," the courier said, holding his salute.

I returned his salute and extended my left hand to take the sealed dispatch. Using my letter opener, I broke the wax seal, which recognized immediately to be Perry's, and unfolded the paper, reading its contents silently:

March 15, 1814

Lieutenant Harris,

You are ordered to vacate the Lawrence immediately, turning her over to the shipwrights to make her seaworthy once again. All wounded men will be transferred ashore to Fort Malden to continue their recoveries. All British prisoners shall be paroled as soon as they are well enough. You will remain with the field hospital as its administrator.

Once seaworthy, the fleet will sail north into Lake Huron under command of Master Arthur Sinclair and commence operations against British forces around Lake Huron. The Niagara, currently under repair in Detroit, will be his flagship. The Lawrence, once repaired and seaworthy, is to return to Misery Bay at Erie, Pennsylvania, and await further orders. You will select an appropriate crew from among the recovering wounded to take the Lawrence to

*Misery Bay. Once the Lawrence has departed, you are
relieved of your command.*

Your Ob't Servants,

O.H. Perry

W. H. Harrison

The orders had been written almost three weeks earlier
and I wondered why it took the courier so long to reach Fort
Malden. He was still standing at attention.

"Soldier, this dispatch is dated almost three weeks ago. Is
there a reason you were delayed in your arrival? Overland,
from General Harrison's headquarters, it should not have
taken you more than a week. Can you explain yourself?" I
said in my sternest command voice.

"Sir. I was taken ill along the way and there was no other
courier who knew the way to this post. It was over a week
before I was well enough to travel," he replied.

"Very well. Please wait here while I draft a reply."

"Of course, sir."

"Are you hungry, soldier?"

"Yes, sir. I have been on hardtack and jerky for a few days
and a hot meal would be most appreciated."

"Report to the mess tent. I am sure they will find something edible for you."

"Thank you, sir."

I felt it was time to give the two commanders a full report of our status, so my reply would take longer than a couple of minutes to compile.

In the report, I outlined the status of our staff, including the addition of White Moon as my wife and the disappearance of Nurse Pritchard in the woods – though I did not elaborate on the circumstances. I also described the status of every wounded man remaining in the hospital and our supply stores.

Finally, I intimated that it was time for me to resign my commission and return to civilian life as there was a baby on the way. As I had already been relieved of command in the latest dispatch, there was no valid reason for me to continue my service.

As I wrote, White Moon entered my quarters. She was beaming.

"Marcus, I felt the baby move inside me just now," she said with absolute joy in her voice. "I cannot yet feel the movements on the outside of my belly, but when I can… you will be able to feel them, too.”

I was speechless. I knew she was pregnant and could see her belly expanding – but had never really grasped that there was indeed a life growing inside her. Until she felt movement, that is. In my previous life, I was often irritated by the younger sailors getting all emotional about seeing their babies in ultrasound exams or feeling them move for the first time. Now the shoe would be on the other foot.

As the courier departed with my reply to the dispatch, I called the two doctors into my quarters. “Doctors, we are to turn the *Lawrence* over to the Detroit shipwrights who will make her ready to sail east to Misery Bay. The *Niagara* will be dispatched north into Lake Huron.”

Continuing, I looked at Doctor Smithwick. “Simon, the orders from General Harrison and Commodore Perry direct me to parole all prisoners once they are healthy. You included.”

“Marcus, I do not intend to return to England. I will remain in Detroit with Christina… Nurse Shelton… as husband and wife,” he responded. “We are still planning on being married as soon as a proper Church of England minister is available.”

"Very well, then. You have made my work easier," I said with a smile.

"Marcus," Wilcox said as he joined the conversation, "Now that Lizzie is gone, there is nothing keeping me here. I thought I would like to remain as a wilderness doctor. Now without a wife or the prospect of one, I am completely bereft of opportunities."

"I appreciate your candor, Stephen," I replied, "but what about your other plans?" I had to talk in innuendo and hoped that he would catch my meaning.

"Oh, that… Yes, I would eventually like to return to where I came from," he said, "but getting there might be challenging."

"Understood. I will do my best to help you travel to wherever you wish to go," I asserted.

I wondered if Stephen Wilcox would eventually find his way back to the oak tree with the carved Hecate's Wheel. He knew it was a time portal and a possible ticket back to his own time. But, without any knowledge of what had happened to Lizzie, I was unsure that he had the fortitude to make another attempt on his own. His vacillation about Lizzie told me that he could be indecisive and weak.

Within a few days of receiving the dispatch from General Harrison and Commodore Perry, a team of shipwrights arrived from Detroit. They quickly set to work on the two brigs, starting with the *Niagara*. It was painfully obvious that, despite my months-long tenure as the commanding officer of the *Lawrence* and the Fort Malden hospital, I was being sidelined. It was time to move on.

23: Jacqui Wilcox
Beginning in April 2018

Jacqui Wilcox had spent the winter with her knight in shining armor, Charles Gordon Bruce. After the frigid mad dash across the Lake Erie ice on his snowmobile, they had become inseparable. Jacqui's often rebuffed, and, by necessity, previously repressed libido got Bruce's attention right from the start. *"She certainly is making up for lost time!"* he thought to himself after one of their extended forays into the bedroom.

With the snow gone and signs of spring emerging, Charles suggested that they drive north to Detroit and visit the Witherell Woods in Palmer Park. As a graduate student in Environmental Studies and Forestry, he had an interest in old growth timberlands in metropolitan areas, especially ones weathering the effects of unconstrained industry. She gladly took him up on the suggestion.

As a precaution after leaving James on South Bass Island, she had reverted to using her maiden name, Blanchet, which was a very common surname in France, her family's homeland. She had studied the language in both high school and college and used it conversationally whenever the B&B

entertained guests from Quebec. Jacqui truly enjoyed opportunities that allowed her to speak her ancestral language.

Riding in Charles's rusting and well-used Pontiac Tempest, it took them about an hour and a half to reach Palmer Park. It was an unseasonably warm day and Jacqui prepared a picnic lunch for them to eat before venturing into the woods for Charles's studies. Because it was a weekday, the park was nearly deserted as were the hiking trails through Witherell Woods. When he was engaged in his academic pursuits, Charles was all business, so Jacqui put any postprandial carnal notions out of her mind – temporarily. She knew it would be "all hands on deck" once they got back home.

After about an hour of traipsing through Witherell Woods on the marked paths, Charles decided that some off-path observation was necessary. Keeping to the trails was not conducive to observing pristine old growth woodlands. He hoped that there was no Detroit municipal ordinance prohibiting off-path exploration.

Taking Jacqui's hand, they climbed a small rock outcropping for an elevated vantage point. At the top, Charles looked off in the distance and spotted a very large oak tree with an ornate circular carving. He pointed it out to Jacqui as something very unusual.

Jacqui was puzzled by how fresh the circle looked. It was much higher off the ground than what high school lovers might have carved to declare their affection for each other.

"Charles, what *is* that carving on the oak tree over there?" Jacqui asked.

"I am not really sure," Charles replied. "It could be something a bunch of teenagers did as a prank."

"I don't think so. It's too high up and too nicely done," Jacqui noted.

"Let's take a closer look, shall we?" Charles said as he took her by the arm and helped her down from the rock.

It took just a couple of minutes for the couple to cross the small clearing. As they crossed, the circle was bathed in sunlight shining through a gap in the canopy. It looked almost freshly carved in the bright sunlight.

"Charles, could you please lift me up so that I can take a closer look at what we are seeing?" Jacqui asked.

Charles was physically fit and in outstanding shape. His regimen of healthy eating and daily exercise left him quite capable of hoisting Jacqui up high enough so that she could investigate the carving.

"Jacqui, why don't you stand on my shoulders? I would appreciate it, though, if you would take those boots off first," he teased, "I don't want footprints on my collarbones."

Jacqui climbed up Charles's back, nibbling his earlobes playfully as she passed. Using the tree for balance, she was quickly standing on his broad shoulders. Her weight was insignificant compared to the power in his muscular legs; in his workouts, he could leg-press twice his own body weight.

Charles slowly stood, giving Jacqui time to adjust her balance. As he did, they both heard a low rumbling like a helicopter off in the distance. The noise was quickly replaced by a vibration that only Jacqui could feel.

"Do you feel that, Charles?" she asked.

"Feel what?" he replied.

"Stop kidding around. I'm serious. Do you feel that?" she asked again.

"I have no idea what you are talking about, Jacqui," he said firmly.

She decided not to press the issue. Perhaps she was just trembling from the uncertainty of standing on his shoulders.

Maybe she was chilled enough to be on the verge of shivering. She just wasn't sure what was causing the perception of vibration.

Reaching the circle, she first touched the middle, marveling at its intricate pattern. Then she put her finger at the bottom dead center of the outer circumference. Upon that first touch, she felt drawn to the carving and did not want to – nor could she – remove her finger. The vibrations became more intense, and the low rumble got even louder.

"Charles!" Jacqui was starting to panic. "I can't move my hand away from the circle."

Her arm suddenly had a mind of its own. She could not resist the force that was causing her finger to trace the circle. It headed from the bottom, counterclockwise towards the top, then halfway down the left side. When her finger reached what would have been due west on a compass, or a heading of 270 degrees, there was a blinding flash.

Charles felt a sudden disappearance of the weight on his shoulders and was hit by a pressure wave from what he thought was an explosion of some kind. He was thrown several feet away from the tree by the pressure wave and he momentarily lost consciousness.

A few moments later, he started to regain his senses and control of his extremities. He stood on wobbly legs, searching the area for any trace of Jacqui. There were no broken branches or disturbed leaves to suggest she was playing a teasing game of hide-and-seek. Normally reserved and unfazed by stressful situations, he began to panic.

"Jacqui? Where are you?" No answer. "This isn't funny. Please come out *now*!" Still no answer. "She has to be someplace nearby," he mumbled as he started to look for her.

About fifteen minutes later, he came across a pile of clothing that looked like it had been quickly removed and dropped in place without any attempt to fold it. It was Jacqui's… right down to the flimsy red lace bra and matching bikini cut panties she had chosen that morning with his approval.

Charles smiled as he saw her clothing, again thinking she was playing some sort of an erotic prank. It wouldn't be the first time she had cavorted naked in a semi-public place, knowing that he could not resist her body and the memory of their almost-public "last time" was more than enough to arouse him. In anticipation of finding her, he undressed as well, compulsively folding his clothes into a neat pile and placing his boots on top. He wasn't a huge fan of being nude outdoors, but he was so smitten by Jacqui that he would do just about anything she suggested or told him outright to do.

*   *   *   *   *

Jacqui woke up and realized that she was naked. *"Hmm… I don't remember undressing. Not that the thought didn't cross my mind, though. Being alone in the woods with that hunk of a man would make any woman want to lose her clothing,"* she giggled internally.

Looking up, Jacqui could see the circle she had just traced her finger around. With no self-consciousness about her nudity, she stood up and found the circle to be within easy reach. When she touched it before, she needed to be on Charles's strong shoulders. Something had changed.

Jacqui was now thoroughly confused. Panic rose through the confusion when she heard what sounded like a human moving through the underbrush.

"Charles? Is that you?" she whispered. "I'm scared."

There was no reply and the crackling she was hearing in the brush abruptly stopped. She now wondered if it was some predator like a bear… or maybe a wolf… determined to make her their next meal. A solitary bear might back down if she showed strength, but wolves traveled and hunted in packs. Against them, she didn't have a chance. Deciding she needed a weapon of some kind, she slowly reached down and picked up a good-sized stick that she could use as a club. It would have to do.

Returning to a fully upright position, she held the club across her body in both hands, nakedness and modesty be damned. Suddenly there was what Jacqui thought was a human female chuckle coming from the bush in front of her. In response, she took a defensive posture with one leg forward of the other; the thought of covering herself never came to mind.

"Come out, whoever you are! My boyfriend is close by and will be here shortly, so don't try anything funny," Jacqui said, trying to mask the fear in her voice.

Out of the bush, a definitely female human form emerged. She was one of the most beautiful women Jacqui had ever seen. Her Native dress made the young woman all the more alluring and mysterious. Jacqui's mind wandered back to those heady college days before she had met James. There was one roommate in particular…

The young woman had a blanket draped over her shoulders. Pointing generally at Jacqui from head to toe, the young woman silently offered the blanket as a cover for her nakedness. Jacqui was so taken by the young woman's beauty that she had forgotten her state of undress.

Jacqui snapped back to reality and ended her previous prurient thoughts when the young woman spoke, asking in both English and French, "Who are you? Where did you come from?" The young woman knew instinctively that Jacqui was not from a Native tribe. Her skin was too white.

"I am not entirely sure," Jacqui replied in English. "My boyfriend and I were… here for a picnic and we were looking at the trees. He is studying Forestry – "

"What is boyfriend? What is this forestry?" the young woman interrupted.

"Forestry is the study of trees and taking care of them," Jacqui answered. She avoided trying to explain the concept of a boyfriend for another time.

"The trees take care of themselves," the young woman giggled, stifling an outright laugh.

"What is your name?" Jacqui asked.

"They call me *Kwekwsé*… Chipmunk… in your words."

"My name is Jacqueline. Jacqueline Blanchet."

"A proper French name. *Parlez-vous Français?*" Chipmunk asked.

"*Oui. Je parle Français comme un natif,*" Jacqui said with a hint of irritation in her voice. Of course, she could speak French like a native; it was the only language her paternal grandparents understood.

"You already know I also speak some English," said Chipmunk.

"My grandmother and grandfather only spoke French, so that is where I learned," Jacqui explained in English."

The rest of their conversation freely switched back and forth between French and English, depending on how comfortable Chipmunk was with the required vocabulary from either language.

Chipmunk explained, "Missionaries and explorers visited our village about one hundred summers ago. They came from France, so naturally taught us their language. The missionaries also insisted that we follow the way of the cross… Christianity, I think you call it, replacing our old ways. Our elders demanded that we keep some of our traditions."

"How interesting," Jacqui acknowledged, "but how did you learn English?"

"An English trapper from… Penn – " Chipmunk stopped, trying to find the right words.

"Pennsylvania," Jacqui interjected.

"Yes, Pennsylvania," Chipmunk confirmed. "That trapper, Jean Hagerty, is my father. He became one of us many summers ago when my mother took him as her husband. He only lives here between planting and harvest. In the winter, he is looking for new places to set his traps. We will be planting soon, so Father should be returning any day."

"*Hagerty?*" Jacqui thought to herself, noticing the French pronunciation of Hagerty's first name. "*Wasn't that the last name of Marcus's Navy buddy? This is really weird.*"

"Your English is very good, Chipmunk. Your father taught you well," Jacqui commented.

"Father told me that someday this land would all be under England and not France and it was important to learn English," Chipmunk replied. "Are you hungry?"

"Yes, I am very hungry, Jacqui replied. She was also suddenly confused about Chipmunk's comment: "under England and not France." She had to have mis-heard Chipmunk's statement. How could her father, John Hagerty, have known or even surmised that such a course of events would transpire?

"Let's go to my village and find you some clothing and food," Chipmunk suggested, taking Jacqui's arm to guide her in the right direction, away from the carved circle and away from anything remotely familiar.

24: Predicaments
April 1814 / April 2018

Now seemingly stuck in 1814, Doctor Stephen Wilcox fell into a deepening melancholy. Bemoaning his predicament and with his only marital prospect gone, he intimated to me that it would be much simpler for him to just wander into the woods and become a hermit or food for the wolf packs that wandered at night.

"No one would mourn my disappearance," he moaned.

I was familiar with this sort of mental state and knew that the best thing I could offer Stephen Wilcox was a nonjudgmental and sympathetic ear. Letting him talk was the best medicine, as long as he did not convey any suicidal ideations.

To encourage Stephen to open up and talk, I had to get him away from the Fort Malden area and into a one-on-one situation. The one thing I would not do would be to take him back into the woods anywhere near where Lizzie had disappeared. Proximity to that situation could easily send him even closer to the edge. Instead, I suggested we take one of the Potawatomi canoes and paddle north towards Detroit under the guise of delivering a document to the shipwrights there. On the water, we could talk without even making eye contact – which I also knew was something that severely depressed individuals wanted to avoid. Once afloat, we fell into an easy rhythm and sporadic but meaningful conversation.

"Marcus, I feel like the world is closing in on me," Wilcox volunteered after we had been paddling in silence for about an hour.

"Why do you say that, Stephen?" I replied.

"First, I get stuck here in this… whatever this place is… and then the love of my life disappears. I don't see a way out of my predicament nor any hope of getting back to my time. I'm tired of what we in 1992 would have called 'meatball surgery,' and not having any medicines to fight infection or disease. How my ancestors did it is beyond me."

"Your ancestors? It sounds to me like you come from a line of doctors," I said, trying to keep him talking.

"Yes," Wilcox replied. "In fact, my fifth great-grandfather treated the wounded at Antietam. Another cousin studied under the watchful tutelage of Dr. Henry Mills Hurd, the first administrator of Johns Hopkins Hospital in Baltimore."

"Impressive. It sounds to me like you have done some research into your family history," I replied. *"Frankly, I couldn't care less,"* I thought, but I had to listen without passing judgment or seeming disinterested.

Wilcox continued, "Some of the things I saw in both the prisoner camp and the regular British Army camp would make your skin crawl. Infections – and amputations, by extension – that could have been prevented with antibiotics or gross vascular surgery. Influenza… no vaccines yet. Lice infestations… again, preventable once permethrin is discovered. It was a physician's nightmare."

Wilcox continued, "Marcus, you came from a time nearly 30 years later than my own. What will it be like, in my future?"

"I'm not sure I should tell you any of this in case you get back to your own time, but…" I paused for effect, "computers and miniature electronic devices are pervasive, and they even have robots performing surgery. In fact, compared to your time, the average person carries more computing power in their pocket than a whole room of computers from 1992. You have so much to look forward to."

"Marcus, I appreciate you not giving me even just a few details. Like you said, it just would not be fair for me to have advance knowledge of things that you already know *will happen* – but from my perspective, they are still in the *may happen* category," Wilcox finally agreed. "All it would take for the progression to change would be for one thing to get out of synch with the rest of the world and *'poof!'* it's the end of the line."

"Exactly," I commented. "Putting it in perspective, it's like that movie where the bully stole the almanac and used it for personal gain. It was one of my favorite movies, but for some reason, I can't remember the title right now."

"Oh, you mean 'Back to the Future'," Wilcox said with a chuckle.

"Yes, that's the one," I acknowledged.

We returned to a more relaxed silence as we focused on the business of paddling. It was one of those idyllic days where the water was flat as glass. For the moment, the only sounds that could be heard were the cacophony of a wide variety of birds and our paddles entering and leaving the water.

I contemplated how much this area would change in the next century and become industrialized when the auto industry under Henry Ford and others would become the dominant factor in the Detroit area – along with the toxic by-products of heavy industry. Now, in 1814, the wildlife was abundant. Bald eagles and osprey soared and dived to the water to catch fish, sometimes fighting over their catch. Deer came down to the water to drink. Natives pulled up nets full of yellow perch and walleye waved as we passed.

*   *   *   *   *

"You! Stop where you are! Police!" a voice bellowed from the trail a little down-slope from where Charles Gordon Bruce was standing. "Keep your hands where we can see them."

Charles had to chuckle at that instruction. He was completely naked without anywhere to hide a weapon. Raising his hands meant he would be immodestly exposed and defenseless. *"Was this another one of Jacqui's pranks?"* he wondered. *"It would be just like her to set up an elaborate scheme like this."*

At first led by their sergeant, the trio of police officers pushed through the brush without regard for the fauna they were trampling. Charles winced as fragile crocuses and emerging lily-of-the-valley plants were crushed by the officers hell-bent on reaching him. The portly sergeant was woefully out of shape and quickly fell behind the other two officers, one of whom was a recent graduate of the police academy, still on probation and in outstanding physical condition.

"Sarge," the academy grad giggled, "this dude's stark naked."

"I can see that for myself," the sergeant replied, somewhat out of breath. "He can stay that way, too, until we figure out what is going on."

"Am I under arrest?" Charles asked.

"You're not the first person to go traipsing through this park naked. It happens quite often and it's a waste of our time to arrest everybody that does," the sergeant replied as he turned to the third officer.

"Grubb?"

"Yes, Sergeant?"

"Begin a circular search radiating out from this position and tell me if you find anything." Officer Grubb nodded in confirmation.

After a few minutes, Grubb shouted, "Sarge, over here!"

"Rookie, guard this man. If he moves, use your taser."

"Yes, Sergeant." The rookie was only a month out of the academy and had not yet so much as drawn the taser from its holster, much less used it on a belligerent suspect.

The sergeant quickly found Officer Grubb in a small clearing. On the ground were both male and female articles of clothing, including some transparent lacy red lingerie, the kind that most men never saw outside of their bedroom.

Officer Grubb knew better than to touch anything he found in the clearing without authorization from a more senior officer. He did notice that the man's clothing was stacked and folded neatly, almost obsessively so, while the woman's clothing was scattered about. Surveying the area once more, Grubb noticed a small purse suspended from a tree branch about 5 yards away.

"Grubb, stay here and don't let anyone or anything disturb the scene. There is no woman anywhere nearby, so I am considering this situation suspicious," the sergeant noted. "I will be right back."

When the sergeant returned to Charles and the rookie officer, Charles asked again, "Sergeant, am I under arrest?"

"Not yet, but you *are* the first naked person we have encountered after finding a woman's undergarments, clothing, and purse scattered in the bushes back there. I think you need to come to the station with us."

"Oh, that… I can explain… The lingerie belonged to my girlfriend – "

"Your girlfriend?" the rookie interrupted. After a brief pause, he asked, "Were you two up to some hanky-panky in the bushes?" The leer on his face did nothing to conceal the rookie's predilection for voyeurism. *"Darn, we just missed the best part!"* he thought.

"That's what I am trying to tell you, officer. She was here one minute, then gone the next. She's completely uninhibited when it comes to being without clothing," Charles explained, hoping to defuse the situation. "It wouldn't be the first time she has cavorted through the woods naked."

"Rookie, radio for the detectives and the crime scene unit," the sergeant ordered, "we need to turn this over to them."

"Yes, Sergeant," the young officer acknowledged as he unclipped the radio microphone from the shoulder of his uniform.

"Dispatch, 1272. We need detectives and CSU to my location, Palmer Park Urban Education Garden. Possible assault and missing person."

"Roger, 1272," the dispatcher replied.

"Rookie, go meet the detectives and CSU at the trailhead, then bring them straight here," said the sergeant.

"Grubb," the sergeant radioed on their team channel, "find this gentleman's trousers and see if there is a wallet in one of the pockets," the sergeant instructed.

"Officer Grubb," Charles pleaded, "my wallet is in the right rear pocket. You will find my Ohio Driver's License under the flap."

"What is your name, sir?" Grubb asked.

"My name is Charles Gordon Bruce. I am a post-doctoral researcher at the University of Toledo. Until I am provided with legal counsel, I am not saying another word. I know how this looks, but you have to believe me that there has been no foul play."

"Then you can explain why we found women's underwear scattered in the bushes," Grubb demanded.

"Like I said, I am not saying anything else until I am represented by counsel," Charles countered. As his clothing was now evidence, he was still wrapped in nothing more than the rookie officer's jacket. "If you insist on keeping me here in the cold, I demand that I be given clothing appropriate for the weather."

"Rookie, take Mr. Bruce to the patrol car, give him a blanket, and keep him there. He should be nice and warm in the back seat. If he has to take a piss, take him away from the unit. It smells bad enough after the drunk we arrested last night."

"Yes, Sergeant," the rookie officer confirmed. Charles groaned audibly as he envisioned the back seat of the patrol car in an unsanitary state and the likely aromas lingering from the night before.

For the next several hours while Charles sat in the back seat of the patrol car behind a plexiglass shield, the Crime Scene Unit, several detectives, and a K-9 unit scoured the area. They were hellbent on finding either a badly beaten woman or a dead body. *"Why else would a woman leave her very expensive lingerie in the woods?"* They all were convinced it had to be foul play. The only clue they discovered beyond the scattered clothing was a small purse with Jacqui's identification and credit cards. At least they now knew who the victim was.

As night fell, the senior detective, O'Brien, called off the search and directed that Charles be placed under arrest.

"Charles Gordon Bruce, you are under arrest on suspicion of murder, the victim being one Jacqueline Wilcox of South Bass Island, Ohio. You have the right to remain silent. Anything you say may be used against you in a court of law. You have the right to talk to a lawyer before answering any questions and to have the lawyer present at any time before or during your questioning. If you cannot afford a lawyer, you may request that the court appoint one for you without charge. Do you understand these rights as I have explained them to you?"

Charles nodded in the affirmative.

"Mr. Bruce, I need your verbal acknowledgement, please," said O'Brien, deadpan.

"Yes, I understand my rights," Charles Gordon Bruce replied.

Handcuffed, Charles was taken to the precinct, given an orange jail jumpsuit, and placed in an interrogation room. As the door slammed shut, Charles hollered, "I am still waiting for an attorney. Until then, don't waste your time trying to get me to talk about anything."

Watching through the two-way mirror, Detective O'Brien was puzzled. In his nearly three decades on the job, he had never encountered anything as strange as this case. He knew he was in for a long night once the public defender arrived.

"Detective, I am Dennis Morris, the public defender assigned to Mr. Bruce's case. May I please have a few minutes alone with my client?"

"Of course, counselor," O'Brien replied as he shut down the audio feed from the interrogation room.

Walking into the room, Morris introduced himself and got right down to business. It took Charles about an hour to explain what he believed had transpired in Palmer Park's Witherell Woods, that it was another one of Jacqui's pranks. He was, however, at a loss to explain the significance of the circle carving on the tree.

"Mr. Bruce, the evidence against you is circumstantial. The police have not been able to locate either an injured woman or a dead body. I will be here with you as long as it takes to convince them that you are not at fault for Ms. Blanchet's disappearance. First, though, we have to get through your arraignment," Morris explained.

"I will tell the judge everything," said Charles, "but I imagine the judge will not believe my recollection of Jacqui's disappearance. It's just all so strange, even to me."

"Do you think you could draw the circle you described?" Morris asked. "I want to be sure it isn't related to her disappearance, perhaps some sort of a gang or human trafficking marker, like dead drops you see in spy movies."

"I can remember that circle as if it were burned into my retinas," Charles said unemotionally.

Fifteen minutes later, Dennis Morris was armed with a sketch of the circle carving. He had studied Greek Mythology as an undergraduate and recognized it immediately as Hecate's Wheel. Hecate, he remembered, was once the so-called guardian of the crossroads and the goddess of magic and sorcery. In his studies, it was never made clear what "the crossroads" might be. *"Perhaps the crossroads is a time portal,"* he thought

"Charles, I think you should let me speak for you. In this instance, less is certainly more. I don't want you to risk being sent for a psych evaluation. We – or I, rather – will stipulate that the lingerie found at the scene was indeed that of Ms. Jacqueline Blanchet Wilcox. We will stipulate that she was estranged from her husband, James Wilcox, currently living on South Bass Island in Lake Erie. We will stipulate that you and Jacqui were involved in a consensual physical relationship."

"Whatever you need to do, Mr. Morris," Charles said.

"I need you to be frank with me now. How did you come to be in association with Ms. Wilcox, a woman nearly twenty years your senior?" Morris asked.

"She was in a mentally and emotionally abusive relationship. Her husband was very demanding, or so she told me," Charles explained. "She used me to discreetly get away from South Bass Island on my snowmobile once Lake Erie had iced over last winter. As far as I know, she has no had any contact with her husband since then."

Morris thought for a moment then asked, "Is there any chance she might have faked her own disappearance and returned to her husband?"

Charles's temper rose in response. "You… stupid… shit," he said loudly, almost screaming, "do you think she took off her clothes and lingerie and ran away – leaving her purse and identification hanging from a tree?"

"If I am to represent you, Mr. Bruce, I have to know the truth. It is also my job to come up with something that will give a jury reasonable doubt of your guilt. If that won't work, a procedural technicality will have to do. Either way, the prosecution will have to prove their case, while all we have to do is convince the judge at your arraignment or the jury at your trial – if we even get that far into the case – that there might be mitigating circumstances, especially if the police can't find a body."

*   *   *   *   *

While Charles was meeting with the public defender, Detective O'Brien tried to call Wilcox's bed and breakfast on South Bass Island. He tried every fifteen minutes for over an hour and decided to call the South Bass Island police department along with the Ottawa County Sheriff's Office. The island's police department did not answer after several attempts, so O'Brien moved on to the Ottawa County Sheriff's Office.

"Ottawa County Sheriff's Office. Deputy Kowalski speaking." Kowalski answered on the first ring.

"Deputy Kowalski, this is Detective O'Brien of the Detroit Police Department. We are investigating the disappearance of one Jacqueline Blanchet Wilcox from Palmer Park here in Detroit. Her identification lists an address on South Bass Island."

Kowalski responded, "What can I do for you, Detective?"

O'Brien continued, "I have tried reaching the South Bass Island Police Department but cannot get anyone to answer their telephone. Are they a seasonal force?"

"Yes, Detective, they are only operational from May 1 to December 1 every year. They will do telephonic "welfare checks" from time to time across the island – which is largely deserted in April."

"We need someone to go to the Wilcox Bed and Breakfast on the island and contact Mr. James Wilcox, Jacqueline Wilcox's husband. We would be very interested to know if his estranged wife had returned home any time during the winter." Detective O'Brien thought it was a reasonable request.

"Detective, the ferries don't start running until May 1, so we would have to send one of our patrol boats out to the island with a pair of deputies. With the weather being what it is right now, that is not likely to happen until at least the day after tomorrow," Kowalski explained.

"I guess that will have to do," O'Brien replied. "I would appreciate a call-back once your team has connected with Mr. Wilcox. Here is my number…"

25: Fort Shelby
April 1814

We reached Fort Shelby just before sunset. The fort was originally named Fort Lernoult when it was built by the British in 1779. It was also known as Fort Detroit from 1805 to 1813. The troops there seemed to be totally despondent and forlorn. They had devolved from military order and discipline and transformed into a rabble of unsavory characters concerned only with self-preservation and survival. We beached our canoe and strode purposefully into the fort.

Major Chadwick, the fort's commanding officer, if you could call him that, was as bereft as the men under him. He had not shaven in days, reeked of perspiration, tobacco, whisky, and urine, and waved lackadaisically when I rendered a proper military salute (despite having resigned my commission weeks earlier). I was truly afraid of what could befall us if we remained within the fort for any length of time. The looks we were getting from the men at the fort suggested other than honorable intentions.

Chadwick did allow us free reign of the post, allowing us to take anything that was needed – as long as we could barter or pay for it in some way. To be honest, I didn't see anything in the fort worth our time or energy – that is, until I went to the remnants of the fort's armory.

The entire time I wandered through Fort Shelby, I felt as if I were being watched or perhaps even clandestinely followed. The feeling was so intense that it made the hairs on the back of my neck stand up. It was a sensation that I had not experienced since a combat engagement in a place that I can't talk about.

A quick review of the cannons staged outside the armory told me that the guns were no longer serviceable. Lack of maintenance had left some unsafe; others had obviously been sabotaged. At the door to the armory – where there should have been an armed sentry – I noticed an abundance of small cannonballs scattered about. They were similar, if not identical, to the ones I had recovered from the bottom of Lake Erie in 2017.

My conversations with Solomon Grimsby, the surveyor, suddenly came flashing back to me. Square pyramidal numbers... the number 204... Was it possible that I could assemble that many cannonballs and invoke the mystical properties to which Grimsby had alluded?

"Wait a minute!" I almost screamed out loud, *"I can't go back to my time. I have a wife and a baby on the way. I cannot... I will not abandon them just for my own selfish desire to go back to 2017."*

My internal dialog went on for several minutes before the solution hit me as forcefully as if I had been punched in the gut by one of the rogues manning the fort. I could send Stephen Wilcox back instead! Granted, it would be about twenty-two years later than it was when he left Connecticut in 1992.

Grimsby's lecture (which I committed to memory) reminded me that 140 was the next-previous square pyramid number – a seven-by-seven structure. It now seemed that we had at least three choices that could jump Wilcox forward in time. Two of those options involved the cannonballs held in Fort Shelby.

The first, to stack the cannonballs in a seven-by-seven square pyramid, would get Wilcox back to 1954. That would be a year before the polio vaccine became widely available and the same year of the first successful kidney transplant. He could use his late 20th Century knowledge to his own advantage.

The second option was what had caused my own jump in time: the eight-by-eight pyramid of 204 cannonballs. I now distinctly remembered stacking each layer in a counterclockwise fashion, thus explaining my backwards jump in time. I believed that Wilcox, though inherently intelligent and a student of progress, would be out of his depth in the fast pace of 2018.

The third option was even simpler. We could return to that circle glyph near the Potawatomi village, where Lizzie disappeared, and try to send him forward to 1994. That would only be two years later than when he left, before the explosion of personal computing technology and more suitable to his current medical knowledge.

I took Wilcox aside and had a whispered conversation with him. "Stephen, I honestly don't trust the men here at this fort. They have lost all sense of honor and military discipline. I do have a couple of ideas I want to discuss with you, but we cannot do it here where anyone could hear us. I propose that we camp for the night near our canoe. With just two of us, having our backs to the water gives us a more defensible position if… when… the so-called soldiers here try to commandeer any of our supplies or weapons."

"I agree with you, Marcus, that remaining here in the fort for the night is probably not our safest option, and even in the low light I can see that several of the men are recovering from smallpox," Wilcox said succinctly. "I am anxious to hear what you have to say, so let's go back to the canoe and have that little talk, shall we?"

In the 20th Century, the courses Sean Hagerty and I had taken in military history and epidemiology during our stateside rotations taught that it was George Washington himself who first mandated inoculation against the dreaded smallpox. The process back then was known as variolation and actually exposed a person to a mild form of the virus. The smallpox vaccination developed by Edward Jenner in England would not become commonplace until the early 19th Century. The global vaccination program carried out for the next 175 years was so effective that in 1980 the World Health Organization declared smallpox to have been eradicated. I was vaccinated as a toddler but did not receive a booster until after I joined the Navy. It was only because of my rating and possibility of deployment to undesirable locations that I was vaccinated again as an adult.

On our way back to the canoe, we stumbled across a rabbit feeding in a small clearing. I dispatched the animal with one well-placed shot. We would be eating fresh meat for dinner and not the questionable jerky we had gotten from Fort Shelby's stores. We decided to only eat the jerky if it was our ration of last resort.

Over our freshly roasted rabbit, I explained to Stephen Wilcox what my suppositions and his opportunities were. Each received a visual response of pursed lips and a pensive short nod. He was most intrigued by the possibility of going forward to 2018, but agreed with me that it might not be in his own best interests to jump headlong into a technology-heavy environment for which he was not prepared. He was also reluctant to go back to the tree carving as it was where he lost the purported love of his life, Lizzie Pritchard.

"Marcus, perhaps I should sleep on it and give you my thoughts in the morning," Wilcox said as we finished our rabbit and washed it down with a shared jug of ale that we had brought along with us from Fort Malden. "I am assuming you want one of us to remain awake and armed all night, so I would like to take the first watch," Stephen offered.

"That would be fine with me. You can wake me in two and a half hours," I replied. My body had long since decided that sleep was necessary. "I hope your pocket watch is wound!"

My assessment of the moral fiber of the men at Fort Shelby proved itself correct about two hours into Stephen's watch. Sensing someone in the bushes near our campsite, he gently prodded me awake. Once again, my combat training kicked in and I instinctively did not vocalize a reply. Though our fire was banked and not much more than embers, I could see Wilcox's hand gestures plainly enough to recognize the indicated direction of the threat.

Slowly and carefully, I slid my hand under my blanket and found the loaded pistol I kept near my right thigh whenever I slept rough. It was at that very second that the bushes exploded with two men charging our campsite. What they weren't expecting was ready resistance.

Two shots rang out, both finding their marks and dropping the men dead in their tracks. When we inspected the bodies, I recognized one of the men as being the one who was nearest the armory. The second was the one who had led us to Major Chadwick's inner sanctum.

Wilcox also quickly looked at the bodies and noticed that they were two of the men he suspected as being smallpox survivors. "Marcus, don't get any closer to those men than you already have. The last thing we need is to carry smallpox with us back to Fort Malden."

"Stephen," I whispered, "never mind that. We need to load up our canoe and leave immediately. Someone at the fort certainly would have heard the shots and we don't have much time before they will be here looking for their missing comrades."

After reloading our pistols, we quickly packed up our gear, loaded the canoe, and pushed off. It would be a long night of paddling, but at least there was enough moonlight to guide our way. We were also aided by the southerly flowing current, so our paddling effort would not amount to much more than steering. With any luck, we would be back at Fort Malden by sunrise, but our hopes for stacking the cannonballs and sending Stephen Wilcox forward in time were now gone.

26: Put-In-Bay Revisited
April 2018

Deputy Tadeusz "Ted" Kowalski was one of the dozen or so deputies in the Ottawa County Sheriff's Office who was certified for all-weather boat operations. He was dispatched to Catawba Island; there, the Department kept two of its patrol and rescue boats in temperature controlled high-and-dry storage. Stored like this, they were ready to launch from a special forklift whenever they were needed – as long as the ice on Lake Erie was in floes and not solid sheets.

Ted Kowalski was joined by Deputy Michael McMaster in the Department's ready room at the marina. They quickly did their pre-launch checks and donned foul weather gear before heading north towards South Bass Island. Fortunately, the weather had abated from the previous days, making it a relatively smooth transit.

In the enclosed cockpit, Kowalski brought McMaster up to speed on what they were supposed to be doing once they reached their destination.

"First, we'll moor at the Put-In-Bay Marina then walk to the Wilcox Bed and Breakfast," Kowalski explained. "When we get there, I hope we will find James Wilcox and his wife, Jacqueline, safe and in good health."

"I hope so, too," was all that McMasters could say. Though he was certified as a rescue boat crew member, he always got seasick on the first patrol of the season, no matter how smooth the water was. This mission was no different. Shortly after Ted finished explaining their mission, Mike left the cabin and was quickly leaning over the side. Ted laughed as his partner lost the contents of his stomach, knowing that Mike would be fine within a few minutes.

Less than an hour later, the deputies were tying the boat off at a reserved slip in the Put-In-Bay Marina. From there, it was just a short walk to the Wilcox Bed and Breakfast. The weather was unseasonably warm, allowing them to remove their foul weather suits before setting off across the green.

Reaching the bed-and-breakfast, Kowalski knocked politely on the door and waited. No answer. He waited a full minute then knocked again on the wooden door using the butt end of his PR-24 side-handle baton. *"It was loud enough to wake the dead,"* McMasters thought. Still no answer.

"Ted, is it possible that there is no one home?" McMasters asked.

"Well… we can always enter the property on the assumption that something suspicious has taken place," Ted explained. "Why don't you try the door?"

It was not unusual for the permanent residents of South Bass Island to leave their doors unlocked during the off-season. McMasters found that to be the case with the Wilcox property: it was unlocked. "Should we go in?" he asked his partner.

"Yes. Let me go first, Mike," Kowalski replied.

Entering the kitchen foyer, Kowalski could see that the house had not been cleaned in quite some time. There were dirty dishes in the sink; they had been left so long that the food waste had congealed onto them. Rodent droppings were present in many areas of the kitchen.

"Remind me *never* to stay here," McMasters said sarcastically.

"Quiet!" Kowalski said harshly. "Do you smell that?"

"Smell what?" McMasters replied.

"Decomp. Something died in here," said Kowalski. "I think we should try to find the source of that stink."

Moving to the front parlor, the sickeningly sweet smell of decomposing flesh was even stronger. McMasters tried a light switch. Nothing. The electricity had been cut off sometime over the winter.

"Let's go upstairs," Kowalski said as he turned on his flashlight.

The bed and breakfast had certainly seen better days. It was as if someone had completely neglected its cleaning and maintenance through the winter. "Ted, it looks to me like no one has even been living here," McMasters noted.

"It does seem rather odd," Kowalski replied as his foot hit the top step. It groaned and creaked loudly as he put the full weight of his 200-lb frame on it. Instinctively, McMaster's hand moved to his holstered Glock, ready to draw it in defense of his partner.

"The decomp certainly has gotten stronger up here," said Kowalski. "We must be getting close."

At the top of the stairs, they had two options: turn left or turn right. The right turn would lead them down a longer corridor; this is where the guest rooms were likely to be located.

Turning left, where the hallway was much shorter, Kowalski surmised that they would be heading to the owners' suite. He was still wondering if the smell might be from dead rodents in the walls. It was not uncommon for rats, mice, or even squirrels to die in the walls of older structures and decompose with the spring thaw. McMasters smelled it, too, and was doing his best to stifle the almost overwhelming urge to vomit – again.

Kowalski's nearly two decades of experience told him that there was a slim possibility that they would be dealing with a double homicide or murder/suicide situation. As the senior officer, he had the choice to lead or follow. He knew that McMasters had not yet dealt with a dead body nor the investigation of an untimely death. It took Ted only a moment to decide.

"Mike, you can take the lead. Please make sure your body camera is turned on," Ted Kowalski reminded. His tone was grim. McMasters took his PR-24 out of his belt with his left hand and kept his right hand on his still-holstered weapon.

At the end of the hall, McMasters found the battered door to James Wilcox's workspace. It still swung freely on its hinges but did not latch as the lockset and jamb had been broken away in James's rage. Reaching the outward opening door, McMasters levered it open with his baton. The door creaked loudly on its hinges as he pushed. With the door now wide open, the airflow of the house changed; both

McMasters and Kowalski were hit with a rushing blast of putrid air. McMasters at least had the presence of mind to remove himself from the room before splattering the floor with vomit. Kowalski, on the other hand, having come from the Cleveland Police Department, was no stranger to scenes such as this. Nauseated, yes, but not retching – yet.

After turning on his own body camera, Kowalski stepped past his partner and entered the office. It looked almost like a "murder board" in the detectives' squad room. Sticky notes, photos, push pins connected by different colored strings, and sheets of handwritten notes were everywhere. Then he saw it: a badly decomposed and partially desiccated corpse sprawled over a mess of papers on a very ornate wooden desk.

Ted decided that they needed to vacate the room and preserve it as a potential crime scene. He did take note of the fact that there was only one corpse, not two as he would have suspected, given Jacqui Wilcox's reported disappearance from that park in Detroit.

A rather quick search of the adjacent room revealed a bedroom that obviously had not been slept in for some time. The dresser drawers were in disarray, as if someone had rapidly packed for a departure, and there were several empty hangers in the closet. Ted noted each of these findings to relay to the detectives when they arrived.

"Mike, you need some air. Why don't you go outside and call dispatch on your cellphone? They will need to send the detectives, Patrol Boat 2, and the coroner," Kowalski noted.

"Yeah, Ted… I'll do that. Anything is better than staying in here with the stiff… and that smell," McMasters replied.

"While you're at it, see if dispatch can give you contact information for the island's police chief. We really should loop him in on this. It's his jurisdiction; we are only here in an advisory, mutual aid situation."

"I'm on it, Ted," was McMasters' reply.

*   *   *   *   *

Less than two hours later, Patrol Boat 2 docked carrying a complement of two detectives, the Ottawa County Coroner, and Fred Miller, chief of the Put-In-Bay Police Department. Because it was off-season, the island's few overwinter residents noticed the unusual arrival. Before the detectives and coroner entered the bed and breakfast, a small crowd had assembled outside. They were not quiet with their gossip.

"I heard his wife left him right after the deep freeze," one voice said.

Another offered, "I heard she was a beaten woman and took her revenge on him."

"I just *knew* there was something suspicious about those two!" another somewhat louder voice asserted.

The detectives had already completed their work in the upstairs bedroom and the coroner was now making his preliminary assessment of the cause of death.

"Gentlemen," Doctor Richards, the county coroner, said as the team assembled in the kitchen out of earshot of the small crowd, "we do not have a homicide on our hands. There is no blood spatter. There is no evidence of foul play. The deceased's skull appears to be intact. It is my preliminary assessment that his death was the result of hypothermia and dehydration. It appears that he has been deceased for approximately three months. Decomposition was slowed by freezing temperatures but accelerated as temperatures became unseasonably warm over the past two weeks."

The coroner continued, "However, I must remind you that, because I have offered a preliminary assessment only, the particulars of this case and your own opinions should not be shared outside of the department and definitely not with the press back on the mainland. Do you all understand?" They all nodded their assent. Richards gave one final verbal barb before closing his notebook: "that includes *you*, Chief Miller."

Chief Fred Miller had a well-deserved reputation for being the town gossip. He always had something to share with somebody about someone on South Bass Island. Keeping anything confidential was a foreign concept to him.

"I will provide my findings in a report after performing an autopsy," Doctor Richards said in closing.

The detectives had already identified the body as one James Kenneth Wilcox, owner and proprietor of the bed and breakfast. They were puzzled by the copious notes and papers strewn about his office. Had James Wilcox been consumed by whatever it was he was researching and simply had a mental health crisis? A potential answer to that question was quick in coming.

Under Wilcox's dessicated left arm, the detectives found a note written in a flourishing script. It appeared to be from Jacqueline Wilcox, the missing woman:

"Dear James,

I can no longer bear the emotional isolation you have brought to our marriage. I am leaving you and this godforsaken island. Do not try to find me.
Good-bye forever,
Jacqui"

"I think we have confirmation that Jacqueline Wilcox is probably alive and well," the lead detective said.

27: It's All About Numbers
April 1814

As we paddled and drifted south, my mind began to wander, and I experienced hallucinations from lack of sleep. In the recesses of my mind, memories of my conversations with Solomon Grimsby kept surfacing and resurfacing. He was the one who explained the concept of square pyramidal numbers to me in a way that even I could understand.

It suddenly hit me like a hammer between the eyes: it wasn't the cannonballs themselves; rather, it was the number of spherical items that enabled the jump from one time dimension to another. I was the one who had made a concrete association with the cannonballs rather than focusing on the number. Was it possible to use other spherical objects to achieve the same result?

As I pondered our situation, I remembered that there was a special type of exploding cast iron shell filled with lead shot – some of which had been in the *Lawrence*'s magazines and bilges. Not generally useful in naval battles against enemy ships, they were held in reserve for shore bombardments intended to disable and demoralize troops inside coastal fortifications.

To use the lead shot from these shells, we would have to crack open the thin iron casing and remove the contents. I wondered if the size of the lead spheres was uniform or random. The only way to find out was to break open one of the shells. For that, we would have to find a very heavy hammer, perhaps from Fort Malden's blacksmith.

"What number did we need? 91? 140? 204? Ninety-one bullets, a six-by-six base, would move the traveler to either 1905 or 1723. A seven-by-seven pyramid needed 140 and would send the traveler to either 1674 or 1954. I had already discussed 1954 with Wilcox: it was probably his best choice. Going back to the 20th Century a few decades earlier than when he had left would work to his advantage. We needed 140 uniformly shaped lead musket balls, pronto.

As dawn broke over the Detroit River, I saw the masts and rigging of the *Lawrence* rising over the horizon. With the new mast in place, the ship would soon be departing for the eastern end of Lake Erie. The orders for the *Lawrence* did not include re-arming it, as the cannon had been removed after the September battle to convert it into a hospital ship and it was Master Commandant Perry's intention to use her as a troop transport.

Were cannonballs still stored in the magazines and on the bilge deck as ballast? It was not out of the range of possibilities. I had never paid much attention to the remnants of the armament at Fort Malden either, having been too preoccupied with the health and welfare of our patients and the imminent repairs to the ships.

"Stephen, once we have had a good meal and some sleep, we need to talk about your future. I have an idea that might work," I said with a wink.

"Marcus, don't tease me like that! The anticipation will keep me from sleeping, which I desperately need to do right now. I am absolutely exhausted," Wilcox replied. He did indeed look the part of a battle-weary soldier and, considering he had killed a man the night before, I owed him some uninterrupted rest.

"I think you are exhausted enough that sleep will come easy for you. Let's talk about it over dinner this evening," I countered. "With any luck, there will be wine or beer for us to drink with our meals. I will leave you undisturbed until dinner time."

I was too excited to sleep though we had been on a very challenging and demanding journey. I needed to get home to my pregnant wife, White Moon, as our child's birth loomed large in our lives though it was still several months away. Stephen had already told me about the childbirth mortality rate in wilderness situations and I certainly did not want to lose either White Moon or our child. Fortunately, Stephen also told me that the Native women were much less likely to die in childbirth than European women and that I need not worry as White Moon was one of the healthiest women he had ever examined.

A few short hours later, Stephen and I met for dinner in the small Officers' Mess as we were both still technically on military duty despite our impending resignations. He looked refreshed but remained pensive; I assumed it was related to our encounter with the two men outside of Fort Shelby and the fact that Stephen had intentionally killed a man for the first time. Even in self-defense, killing a man was not something to be taken lightly.

"Stephen, I have a proposition for you," I said to open the conversation. There was no one else in the mess except for an orderly who was tending to the soup pot.

"What might that be, Marcus?" he asked.

"If we could send you forward to 1954, would that be acceptable?"

"I think it would certainly be better to re-live a period in time with future knowledge than it would be to live in the future and having to catch up," Wilcox replied.

"Then we had best get busy…" and I spent the next hour explaining to him how we could help him make the jump forward in time.

I gave Wilcox a very long and detailed explanation of what we needed to do to assemble the requisite number of bullets. I then told him it was my belief that the direction of stacking, clockwise or counterclockwise, was what enabled a person to jump forward or backward in time. He agreed with that logic and was willing to place that last bullet on top of the miniature pyramid, just like I had done at Put-In-Bay for the re-enactment in 2017.

Breaking open the six shells we found belowdecks on the *Lawrence* was easy, but the revelation of their contents was disappointing. No two lead balls within the casings were the same size; it was as if molten lead had been dribbled into a barrel of cold water and had cooled into irregular spherical shapes. We would have to melt them down and somehow recast them into more uniform spheres.

The answer was bullet molds! A remnant of military equipment from the American Revolution, each soldier carried one in his kit, along with a copper melting pot, to make new bullets whenever materials were available. It was not uncommon for soldiers to turn bullet-making into a social activity and an opportunity to relax from the challenges of encamped military life. Wilcox had managed to acquire ten bullet-making kits from soldiers who had perished under his care.

All through the night it was a tedious cycle of melt-pour-cool-melt-pour-cool. Towards dawn, the giddiness of sleep deprivation set in, and Wilcox was hardly able to contain his exuberance. Recognizing that he was again exhausted. I suggested that preparing for time travel was certainly not for the weary and that sleep would be appropriate. Doctor Stephen Wilcox readily agreed.

The next morning, after a later than normal rising and a hearty breakfast, I prepared to say goodbye to Stephen Wilcox yet again. We gathered the musket balls we had made the night before and found a quiet place to stack them, out of sight of the rest of the fort. First, we laid a seven-by-seven perimeter for the base layer, orienting the square so that each corner pointed in a compass direction, starting with north and working clockwise through east, south, and west. With the perimeter laid, we filled in the rest of the base.

Working in a similar fashion for the next layers, we eventually reached the penultimate layer. Wilcox was trembling with anticipation as only one musket ball was needed to complete the apex of the pyramid. He was afraid that his tremors would cause inadvertent contact and make the whole pyramid collapse.

As Wilcox moved his hand over the nearly completed pyramid, I wondered if he would experience the same sensations I had before I was transported back to 1813. As far as I knew, my jump backwards in time was instantaneous once the final ball was in place, but I did experience some weird sensations as I lifted that final cannonball to the top of my own pyramid. I chose not to provide Wilcox with any information on what to expect, as his experience could be completely different than my own.

Wilcox's hand hovered over the pyramid's apex. His eyes locked with mine for what seemed like an eternity before he stared at the pyramid to fix the positioning of the final musket ball in his mind. He inhaled and exhaled deeply, like he was meditating at the end of a yoga practice, then inhaled once more and held his breath. Slowly closing his eyes, his hand drifted downward and gently placed the final musket ball before drifting back up and away from the geometric shape. It was an almost otherworldly experience.

After about a minute, Stephen Wilcox opened his eyes and saw that I was still there. "Did anything happen, Marcus?" he asked. I could see he was disappointed that I was still there with him.

"I don't think so," I replied. "Did you feel anything unusual as you placed the last ball? Perhaps a weird out-of-body sensation or an unseen force drawing your hand towards the pyramid?"

"Neither one, Marcus. I didn't sense anything of the kind," he answered.

'Strange. I thought our efforts would have taken you to 1954 like we expected."

"Well… *obviously*, it didn't work," Wilcox said dejectedly, "as I am still here with you."

"Were there any strange sensations as your hand approached the pyramid with that final ball? Perhaps an aura of blue light?" I asked.

"No. Nothing at all," Stephen Wilcox replied, the frustration in his voice obvious.

It seemed odd to me that he did not experience any of the unique sensations I had when I stacked number 204 on the top of my cannonball pyramid. Aside from the size of the spheres and the direction in which we laid down the musket balls, we had recreated the conditions of my own jump backwards in time. We both believed that the number of objects and their configuration into a square pyramid were the mathematical catalysts for time travel.

What was I missing? There had to be something. I didn't remember anything between placing the final cannonball on my own pyramid in 2017 and being conscious of a naval officer barking orders in 1813. It could be something before or after my timeline change. I had no idea what it was.

"Stephen, what do you remember about your own jump backwards in time?" I asked.

"Like I told you before, it seemed to have something to do with that ornate circle in the church basement... the catacomb I told you about. Hecate's Wheel," he answered.

Then it hit me: the commonality between my pyramid and his was the strange marking on the final cannonball in my pyramid. It wasn't a foundry marking after all; rather, it was a miniature engraving of Hecate's Wheel. *That* was the key! It was the only thing common to Lizzie's disappearance, Wilcox's original jump, and my own sudden appearance in 1813.

Could we duplicate the wheel on the final musket ball for Wilcox's pyramid? I certainly did not have the skills and neither did he. We would have to retain the services of an expert engraver to carve the wheel on that final musket ball, a little less than three-quarters of an inch in diameter. Was there such an engraver within a day's ride from Fort Malden?

I decided to ask Doctor Smithwick and Nurse Shelton if they could help locate such a craftsman.

The area surrounding Fort Malden, known as Amherstburg, was still a frontier town that had changed hands several times since the war began. It would be another sixty-plus years before it was incorporated as a municipal jurisdiction. Regardless, Christina Shelton assured me that yes, there was indeed an expert engraver in the vicinity, a Jewish man whose family had come from Montreal during the Seven Years War. Everyone simply knew him as "Franks." No first name. Just "Franks," or maybe "Mister Franks" upon first meeting.

"Christina, do you know where we can find this 'Franks' person?" I asked.

"Yes, Marcus. He has a shop not far from the fort. We can go there tomorrow if you like."

"Yes, that would be fine," I acknowledged. "We will be on our way just after breakfast."

28: Little Circles
April 1814

With Christina Shelton's help, we quickly located Franks's establishment. It was just a small storefront with cottage living quarters in the rear. The shop was clean and very well-kept. It gave me a sense that Franks would be a perfectionist and meticulous in anything that he did.

Hearing the bell on the door announce our entry, Franks came out of the back room. He was wearing a yarmulke and had tassels affixed to his waistcoat. His shuffling gait and stooped shoulders gave him a humble, deferential appearance. Franks was indeed a Jew – a rare occurrence in North America in the early 19th Century.

"Mister Franks, I am Lieutenant Marcus Harris of the United States Navy. The gentleman with me is Doctor Stephen Wilcox and I believe you already are acquainted with Nurse Shelton," I began. I used my rank as my military situation was still in limbo: I had not heard back from Master Commandant Perry nor General Harrison that my resignation had been accepted. "If we draw something for you, could you engrave it on a lead musket ball?"

"That's an awfully small work surface and it is round," he said, "making it very difficult, but not so difficult that it cannot be done. Lead is very soft and can be easily engraved with the proper tools. And… now that we have met, you may simply call me 'Franks'. There is no need for the formality of 'mister.' Can I offer you anything in the way of refreshment?"

"Franks it is, and a tankard of ale would be wonderful," I acknowledged. He had an accent that was not what I would have expected for someone from Montreal.

"Doctor Wilcox will draw what we need," I said. "Stephen, will you do the honors, please?"

"Franks, might I take advantage of your quill and inkpot?" Wilcox asked.

"But of course! Do you also require paper?" Franks replied. Stephen nodded and grunted in confirmation and the paper quickly appeared on the worktable. Franks then disappeared to gather our drinks. We could hear a muted discussion between him and a female voice, in what I assumed was Yiddish, coming from the back room.

With the paper positioned in a spot of bright sunlight, Stephen quickly completed an elaborate representation of the glyph he had seen both on the tree in the Michigan woods and on the wall in the New Haven church basement. I confirmed that it was an accurate facsimile of the tree carving. As Stephen handed me his sketch, I noticed that his right hand was trembling once again. I didn't know if it was nerves or an after-effect of the circle. After all, it was the tree carving that presumably sent Lizzie Pritchard somewhere else in time. My hope was that Lizzie was alive and well and living in 1634.

My mood and reminiscence were interrupted by Franks's whiny, high-pitched voice. He offered our drinks and then looked at Stephen's drawing.

"But of course! It is Hecate's Wheel from Greek mythology," Franks exclaimed. "I can engrave that on a musket ball as you requested. It is no more difficult, really, than engraving a locket."

"Franks, should we leave you alone so you can work?" Stephen asked.

"That isn't necessary, Doctor Wilcox. It won't take me very long. I would appreciate it, though, if you had an extra ball just in case I make an error with this one," Franks said.

When Stephen and I had cast the musket balls, we made sure that we had produced more than the 140 needed to move him forward to 1954. As a precaution and for my own return to what now would be 2018, should that become necessary, we had cast an extra 65 balls – one more than I would need for my own pyramid.

"Gentlemen, please sit. Make yourselves comfortable. I work better if my customers give me some space," Franks said with a grin, "but I rarely ask them to leave the shop while I work."

Franks then placed the ball on a block of oak in which a small depression had been hollowed; there was a glob of sticky beeswax in the bottom of the depression. Franks needed that to help hold the ball in place while he worked. He was a most cheerful fellow, whistling and humming softly to himself as his tools scraped away a thin layer of the soft lead.

Our ales, which were more like a fortified wine than ale, were barely half gone when Franks informed us that he was done. It had taken less than an hour.

"How did you do that so quickly?" Stephen asked.

"A master engraver knows certain tricks," Franks replied, "I have been doing this for nearly thirty years."

"Outstanding work," I added to the conversation. "How much do we owe you for your efforts, Franks?"

"That will be one American dollar," he replied. "I no longer accept British money."

I reached for my money purse as Franks gingerly wrapped the engraved musket ball in a small square of tanned rabbit pelt, fur side touching the ball. He began to hand it to me, but Stephen reached out and intercepted the transfer, snatching the ball from Franks's hand.

"Not so fast, Marcus. You may have paid Franks, but the ball is… well… you know…"

I glared at Stephen Wilcox as I struggled to control my anger. I could tell that he did not trust me and expected that I would use the engraved ball to facilitate my own time travel, not his. His presumption couldn't have been more wrong; there was no way I was leaving White Moon and our child behind in the 19th Century.

Throughout this current ordeal, beginning with Lizzie Pritchard's disappearance, Wilcox had become nothing but trouble, a burr under my saddle. Though I wanted him gone from 1814 as quickly as possible, his snatch-and-grab behavior was annoying and petulant. I truly hoped that the engraving would work to activate the mystical powers of the ball as it was placed on top of the pyramid.

After I paid Franks, we left the shop in silence. The tension between us had risen significantly in the last hour. I hoped it would be one of our last together.

*　*　*　*　*

We returned to Fort Malden a short while later and were met by Smithwick and Christina Shelton, who had returned to the fort after showing us where Franks had his shop; she felt it unnecessary to wait with us while we went about our business.

My first concern after my return was for White Moon's wellbeing. She had been afflicted with morning sickness of late and, in spite of her healthy composition and lifestyle, it was debilitating. Christina told me in her most matronly tone that my wife was resting comfortably in our quarters and should not be disturbed. I nodded my agreement.

"Were you successful?" Smithwick asked.

"Yes, we were," Wilcox replied. He pulled the polished musket ball out of his pocket, gingerly unwrapped it from the rabbit fur, and showed it to the couple.

"Franks certainly does fine work," Christina noted. "He is well known for his ability to work magic on very small surfaces. I do have one question, though: why was it necessary to have that… whatever it is… engraved on a musket ball, of all things?"

Wilcox and I looked at each other, our faces devoid of expression. I nodded my agreement that he should speak first. It would then be up to me to validate whatever he said.

"I had this made as a gift for Lizzie when she comes back. I am sure she will like it," Wilcox explained.

"Yes, I am sure she will," I confirmed.

Christina Shelton was skeptical. She pursed her lips and I could almost feel her thoughts, the most obvious of which likely was, *Why would any self-respecting woman want a gift like this? It really would have to be love for her to accept it.*

About this time, White Moon joined us from her rest. She, too, was shown the engraved musket ball, but her reaction was dramatically different than Christina's.

"Marcus, it is beautiful! Did Stephen have it made for Lizzie in case she comes back?" White Moon asked.

My eyes darted back and forth between White Moon and Stephen Wilcox. Whatever my answer, Stephen had to support it. I chose to defer.

"Stephen?" I queried.

"Yes, White Moon, I had it carved for Lizzie in hopes that she will find her way back to me. I thought the carving to match where we last saw each other was a fitting tribute to our love," Stephen responded.

Christina Shelton was a little… a lot… less melodramatic and quite cynical. "Looks like a cheap piece of lead to me. Seems to me that if you truly loved her, Stephen, you would have had something made of gold or silver – certainly not a lead musket ball." The icy tone in her voice cut like a dull knife through a tough steak..

I was worried that Stephen might let it slip that the polished and engraved musket ball was not a gift all. We had to send him on his way sooner rather than later. His mood swings were starting to wear me down and I had more important things to deal with – like a pregnant wife.

The small talk with Doctor Smithwick and Nurse Shelton lasted about another fifteen minutes. It was mostly about patients and concerned Doctor Wilcox more than it did me. I was technically still in charge of the hospital and Fort Malden while awaiting the final separation order from General Harrison or Master Commandant Perry, but my involvement in day-to-day operations had become almost nonexistent over the past two or three weeks.

Wilcox finally extricated himself from the conversation and turned to me, speaking almost in a whisper, "Marcus, I want to try again – today – as soon as the sun goes down. Do you have the rest of the musket balls handy?"

"Yes, Stephen. They are in a leather pouch in my quarters. Once White Moon wakes from her nap, I will fetch them and be ready whenever you are," I replied. "As a doctor, I am sure you understand how pregnant women need their rest."

Though I was not the one contemplating time travel, my mind was still racing. Would Wilcox go through with it this time? Would he survive? Would all the effort we put into the musket balls pay off? I wanted this to be over just as much as Stephen Wilcox did.

It was nearly an hour before White Moon awoke from her nap. It was completely out of character for Potawatomi women to take time off from their often grueling day unless they were really ill – and this was one case where illness, even something as normal as morning sickness, had won.

"White Moon, my darling, are you rested?" I asked when she emerged from our quarters.

"Yes, Marcus. The sick feeling has passed and I really should get something to eat," she replied.

"It's nearly dinner time," I noted, "we should be able to find something to eat in the mess tent shortly. Until then, I have a fine loaf of sourdough bread I brought back with me from our trip this afternoon. Perhaps that will help settle your stomach even more. If that doesn't work, Mrs. Franks gave us some very good ginger snap cookies, too."

"That would be wonderful, my husband," she said with a smile, "bread and ginger snaps settle my stomach."

"The baked goodies are the only real gifts we brought back," I explained, "and you already know that Stephen was not truthful about the engraved musket ball…"

*   *   *   *   *

The evening meal was one of the strangest I had ever taken with Stephen Wilcox. Because he had been a prisoner before the British quit Fort Malden, he usually kept to their discipline of prisoner silence during meals. It had become a habit; he rarely spoke while eating, waiting until after the detritus of the meal had been cleared away by our orderlies, loosening up only after a tankard of ale or glass of wine.

Tonight was different. Wilcox was animated and conversant about anything and everything. He was so full of nervous energy that I compared him to a child returning home from a visit to grandma's house and the sugar-laden cookie jar. White Moon, too, noticed the change in his behavior and wondered what had caused such a change.

I turned to her and whispered, "Tonight is the night. Everything is ready and we will be trying to send him away, forward in time, to 1954."

"Would you like for Running Deer and me to stand watch while you get everything ready?" she asked.

"I think that would be a good idea," I agreed, "and we need to find a place that is out of sight from the rest of the camp. Who knows what might happen when he stacks the last musket ball on top of the pyramid."

"Well, we could always go back to the clearing where Lizzie disappeared," White Moon suggested. "You already told me the symbol carved into the tree and the one on the last cannonball in your pyramid are connected."

I squeezed White Moon's hand to signal a pause in our conversation as the orderly cleared the dinner plates away. Orderlies were the gossip mongers of military camps and ours were no different. Anything an orderly learned would be all over the camp in a matter of a few hours.

With the orderly out of earshot, I responded to White Moon's suggestion. "I don't think that would be a good idea, my darling. Stephen has been loathe to even speak of her since she disappeared," I said as empathetically as I could.

29: The Blue Flash
April 1814

We secreted ourselves away from the rest of the camp in a small clearing at the edge of the forest and the beginning of the path that led to the Potawatomi's riverside fishing village. Very few of the soldiers or camp followers ever went on that path at night as the more superstitious of them considered the forest to be haunted. The reality, though, was that they were hearing the sounds of owls, coyotes, foxes, and catamounts calling out in the night.

Our chosen site to send Stephen Wilcox to 1954 was behind a waist-high stone and brick wall just to the east of the woodland path's beginning. The wall surrounded the vegetable gardens planted by American prisoners before the hasty British departure the previous fall and obscured us from the rest of the fort. We felt certain that discovery was unlikely.

With Running Deer and White Moon standing watch in both directions – her facing the camp as she peered over the wall and him watching the trail – we were ready. All we were lacking was Stephen Wilcox; I had already retrieved the bag of musket balls from my quarters. The specially engraved one with the glyph had not left the rabbit fur pouch in my pocket since I took it back from Wilcox for safe keeping: I wanted to be certain that it did not get lost. It would remain there until Wilcox was laying the penultimate layer of the pyramid.

When Wilcox arrived, nearly half an hour after us, he was still full of excess nervous energy and suffering from a severe case of diarrhea of the mouth, as we would say in the 20th Century. I hoped he would quickly quiet himself and focus on the business we had before us. He needed to concentrate and free his mind of all distractions other than stacking the musket balls and placing the final engraved ball at the top of the pyramid. He had to go through with it. He certainly could not stay here in 1814.

Wilcox was dressed in attire very similar to that of President Andrew Jackson in a portrait I had once seen in the Smithsonian American Art Museum nearly 200 years in the future. We had already established that clothing from the future might not survive a time hop, but clothing from the past was always in vogue– especially for costume parties. He looked simply grand in the black and white ensemble of frilly shirt, cravat, black tailcoat, and knee-length trousers. His boots were polished to a sheen. He was ready.

I noticed, too, that Wilcox was carrying a black leather medical bag. It was the kind we all associated with "house call" doctors on TV in the 1950s and 1960s. I wondered how he came up with the bag, considering he had arrived in 1813 naked as the day he was born. Then I remembered that he had told me about the bag being his only connection to where he came from.

Getting back to the task at hand, I used my pocket compass to determine north, then drove small sticks into the soft forest earth to mark the other three compass points. Logic – and Solomon Grimsby – suggested that starting with north to represent the present and working clockwise from there would enable forward time travel. I showed Wilcox where to place the first musket ball. He pressed it gently into the soft earth, placing the next six balls in a line heading diagonally towards the east.

I guided Wilcox in this manner, making a seven-by-seven diamond shape. From this perimeter, he filled in the remainder of the base, using up 49 balls. Compared to my cannonballs seven months earlier, this pyramid was miniscule. According to the surveyor, Solomon Grimsby, the overall size did not matter – just the number of balls stacked to complete the square pyramid.

So that Wilcox's efforts would not be diluted by the touch of another person, I had dumped the other musket balls out of the pouch onto a firmly packed square of dirt. Once the stacking started, he was the only one who would touch the balls. I would guide his placement, for sure, but touching anything other than the guide stakes I had already placed could be dangerous to us all. We all remembered how Lizzie suddenly disappeared when she traced the tree carving under Wilcox's duress. I didn't want that to happen to me, nor did I want to do *anything* that would impede Wilcox's departure.

Slowly and methodically, Wilcox moved to the second level. This one needed 36 balls to complete. Unlike the base layer, more caution was necessary to ensure that the balls did not roll off the pyramid once they had been placed. I noticed Stephen Wilcox's hand trembling as he worked his way to the center of the layer.

With the second layer now in place, Wilcox looked at me and raised his eyebrows as he cocked his head to one side. It was as if he was afraid to speak, but I understood his gesture to mean that he needed to take a break from his efforts. Remembering back to my own experience on South Bass Island, I knew it would not make a difference if there was a gap in time from one layer to the next; after all, I had to wait for James and Sean to deliver each load of cannonballs from the salvage yard near the marina.

By the time Wilcox got to the fourth layer and its sixteen musket balls, I was sensing a spreading warmth in my jacket pocket. It reminded me of the chemical handwarmers we used to keep in our equipment bags for night operations during my 20th Century Navy days. The warmth probably started spreading with the second or third layer, but I was too focused on what Wilcox was doing to notice.

Knowing that the warmth in my pocket was an indication of *something*, I removed the rabbit fur pouch and placed it on the ground between Wilcox's knees. He nodded in acknowledgment, knowing exactly what needed to be done with the engraved sphere.

As he placed the final ball in the fifth layer, I began sensing a low frequency rumble like a subway train rolling through a tunnel beneath our feet. Unlike the subway, though, there was no quivering or shaking – just noise. White Moon and Running Deer both looked at me with concerned expressions but remained speechless as they, too, did not wish to interrupt Wilcox's concentration.

With the sixth layer now in place, all that remained was the engraved ball. Wilcox reached down between his knees for the rabbit fur pouch and removed the lone ball – which was now almost hot to the touch. His eyes widened as the rumbles increased again in volume.

"Can you hear that, Marcus?" Wilcox asked.

"Yes, Stephen, I can. It is nothing to be afraid of… Remember the last time we tried to send you away? There was nothing. No sound. No vibration at all," I replied.

Slowly and purposefully, he took the final ball in his right hand and guided it to its resting place at the top of the pyramid. A look of panic suddenly spread over his face.

"Marcus! I can't stop! It's pulling me. How can something this small exert such a force and overcome my resistance?" he asked.

"Just relax and let things happen," I countered, trying to retain a comforting tone in my voice. His hand was now less than six inches away from the apex of the pyramid.

When his hand was about half an inch away from the apex, an unseen force took over, locking Wilcox's fingers around the final musket ball. The ball made the apex of the pyramid with a solid *"clack!"* that reminded me of the tumblers in a door lock falling into place. Concurrent with the sound of that final ball being pulled into place, there was a blinding blue flash like a lightning bolt and a concussive force like an exploding hand grenade. I was thrown back into the woods several yards. Running Deer, too, was knocked over. White Moon later would explain to me that she was pressed against the wall but not so violently that she nor our baby were injured. We were all dazed to some degree.

When I looked at the musket ball pyramid, there was a small column of smoke rising from it and Stephen Wilcox was nowhere to be seen. It looked like he had finally made the jump. *"Good riddance,"* I thought to myself.

"White Moon, are you hurt?" I called out.

"No, husband, I am fine, and our baby just kicked me."

"Were you thrown against the wall?" I asked, somewhat fearing the answer.

"It was strange," White Moon began, "I felt safe and secure, as if an unseen being was protecting me. Yes, I was pushed towards the wall, but not in a way that would have injured me."

Running Deer joined the conversation. "Sister, Marcus… I was thrown into the woods when Doctor Wilcox disappeared. I was dazed but unhurt."

"I think we should take that pyramid apart and keep the engraved ball in a safe place," I suggested.

"Marcus, if you keep it, how can I trust that you won't try to go back to your own time?" White Moon asked; in the moonlight, I could see tears welling up in her eyes.

"I have told you before, my darling, that I will not leave you or our baby behind. If the time is right for me to return to where I came from, you will be right there at my side," I said tenderly, taking her hand in mine. "I hope I never have to decide when that right time is."

Wilcox had not yet been gone five minutes when we heard Doctor Smithwick and Christina Shelton running towards us from the infirmary. They, too, had seen the blue flash.

"Marcus, are you alright?" Smithwick asked.

"Yes, Doctor. We are all unhurt," I answered.

Christina looked at White Moon. "And the baby?"

"I just felt it kick, so all is well," White Moon beamed.

Smithwick's observant nature kicked in. "We saw a flash of lightning, but there is barely a cloud in the sky… I've heard of such a phenomenon before. I think it is called 'St. Elmo's fire.' Mariners believe it is a favorable omen."

Was it time to tell Doctor Smithwick and Nurse Shelton about our time-traveling adventures? I knew that Smithwick would not accept on face value an explanation that it was lightning; he was, after all, a man of science trained in one of the best medical institutions in the world.

Nurse Shelton, on the other hand, had proven to be just as superstitious as some of the soldiers. My mind could already hear the accusations of "witchcraft!" coming from her mouth. She was a good nurse as she cared for the sick and wounded but was not highly educated. She could read, write, and do simple arithmetic – but abstract concepts beyond her faith in God Almighty were usually dismissed out of hand. I decided that including her in my explanation was not in our best interests.

"Doctor Smithwick, a word, if I may?" I said with a soft nod to the side to indicate I wished to speak with him privately.

"Of course, Lieutenant Harris," he replied.

"White Moon, Running Deer, will you see Nurse Shelton back to her quarters, please?" I asked over my shoulder as Smithwick and I went a few yards into the woods.

Once I was sure we were out of hearing distance, I quietly spoke to Smithwick. "Simon, you are an educated man," I began, "have you ever considered that time travel might be possible?"

His look changed from inquisitive to bewildered. "I am not really sure, Marcus. I am not a man of faith, instead choosing to follow a more analytic approach, accepting the concept of *debet esse probandum,* or 'it must be proven.' In other words, I need proof."

"Simon, you will just have to trust me. Thomas Wilcox has left us," I stated to start my explanation.

"Left us? What do you mean, 'left us?'"

"Do you see that stack of musketballs over there?" I asked.

"Yes. Perhaps it was some soldiers' drinking game – to see who could place the final one on top even when falling-down drunk," Smithwick offered.

"Simon, listen to me… It was not a soldiers' drinking game. There's more to this story and if you will stop trying to analyze everything in scientific terms, I will tell you all about it."

"Go on," Smithwick said as he took a seat on a fallen log. As he would any other time he was deep in thought, Simon absentmindedly stroked his chin with the fingers of his right hand.

"As I was saying, Doctor Wilcox is no longer with us. If our calculations were correct, he should now be safely back in the future, most likely 1954."

"That's preposterous!" Smithwick bellowed.

"There's more… I, too, am a time traveler. I came from the Year of Our Lord 2017," I said, maintaining constant eye contact with Doctor Smithwick, whose agitation was growing by the second.

"How can this be?" Smithwick asked.

"There seem to be certain mystical powers in things like square pyramids and symbols from Greek Mythology –

especially when the two are combined." I paused to let this idea sink in.

"What symbols are you talking about?" Smithwick asked.

"I want you to go over to that stack of musket balls and take one of the corner balls from the third layer before the apex." It was my intention for him to cause the pyramid to collapse, as I did not know if the final, engraved ball was still connected to am open time portal.

"Why not just take the top one?" he asked.

"The top one is what makes time travel happen. As it is placed, the person holding the ball is sucked into the portal and '*poof!*' they are transported to another time. I am not sure if that power remains after the person is gone – so you will cause part of the pyramid to collapse if you take one from a corner further down. Then, and only then, do I feel it would be safe for you to touch the engraved ball from the apex." My explanation had suddenly become long-winded and focused only on Wilcox's situation with no further mention of my own. That would be my next task, to explain where I came from and how I got here.

30: Doctor Stephen Wilcox
Amherstburg, beginning in April 1954

The intersection of Sandwich and Fort Streets in Amherstburg was unusually busy that evening. Traffic was stop-and-go and pedestrians scurried between the barely moving cars. It took several cycles of the traffic lights on Sandwich for the traffic to clear.

Young Jimmy Simcoe dashed into the intersection just as an inattentive driver missed the red light. A screeching of brakes was followed by a dull thud as the 1947 Packard struck Jimmy with enough force to propel him several feet forward. A crowd quickly gathered around the child and a remorseful driver who attempted to render assistance to the unconscious child.

Just a split second after the impact, there was a blue flash that none of the onlookers even noticed. Doctor Stephen Wilcox had arrived – fully clothed. Aside from being slightly disoriented, he was none the worse for wear. Looking at signage on a storefront, he determined that he was still in Amherstburg, Ontario, Canada and presumably not too far away from Fort Malden.

As his disorientation cleared, Wilcox sensed that something was amiss in the intersection ahead and he strode purposefully toward the crowd.

A very attractive young woman looked quizzically at his attire, then noticed the medical bag in his left hand.

"Sir, are you a doctor?" the woman asked.

"Yes, young lady, I most certainly am," Wilcox replied.

"You look like something out of a history book," the young woman giggled.

"Young lady… I have just come from…" Wilcox paused for a moment to collect his thoughts and deliver a plausible reason. "I have just come from a fancy dress cocktail party."

"Do you see that crowd?" the young woman asked.

"How could I miss it?" he replied.

"A boy was struck by a car and I think he's badly hurt. Come quickly, please!" She took Wilcox by the hand and led him towards the accident.

A few seconds later, they arrived at the outer edge of the dense crowd encircling the Packard and the still unconscious boy. As the young woman pushed through the crowd with Doctor Stephen Wilcox in tow, she repeated, "Make room for the doctor, please." Each repetition brought with it a greater stridency.

Wilcox knelt beside the child and did a quick assessment of his condition. He had a strong pulse and was breathing quite normally. The boy's pupils responded equally to light; that ruled out massive brain trauma. A head-to-toe pat-down revealed no grossly broken bones and a palpation of the child's abdomen suggested no internal bleeding.

"Who is the driver of this car?" Wilcox demanded.

A very shaken woman on the verge of tears identified herself as the driver. Wilcox got close enough to her that he could smell alcohol on her breath.

"What is your name?" he asked her.

"Velma… Velma Schnaubelt," she answered.

"Miss Schnaubelt… or is it *Mrs.* Schnaubelt? You are very fortunate that this young lad was not seriously injured. He might have a concussion and a headache for a few days – but no bones, thankfully, are broken and he has sustained no discernible internal injuries."

"Oh, praise Jesus!" the woman exclaimed, again a cloud of alcoholic vapors wafting from her mouth. "And it is *Miss* Schnaubelt, Doctor."

"Miss Schnaubelt, I strongly suggest that you turn yourself over to the police when they arrive and that you seek out the boy's parents to apologize for injuring their son. I believe that your drinking contributed to this accident." Wilcox's tone was firm and commanded obedience.

"Yes, Doctor," Velma Schnaubelt replied apologetically.

Hearing the whine of approaching police sirens and the slightly deeper sound of an ambulance siren, Velma Schnaubelt suddenly became quite agitated and was approaching panic.

"Doctor, please don't tell them I was drinking. I already have a record with the police department. They warned me last time that I could go to jail if I ever hurt anyone after I'd been drinking," Velma pleaded as she squeezed my upper arm.

"Miss Schnaubelt, you know I am ethically bound to make a full report to the authorities when they arrive," Wilcox explained, "and this situation is no different." His no-nonsense tone reduced Velma Schnaubelt to tears almost instantly.

At just that moment, the ambulance pulled up. Wilcox had to smile: it was a 1950 Chevrolet 150 ambulance – nothing more, really, than a station wagon with a rear-facing half-seat next to a stretcher platform. By 1990s standards, it was archaic and really only useful for patient transport, not emergency triage and treatment as would become the norm just a couple of decades later. Wilcox had to stifle a laugh as the so-called ambulance reminded him of "Ghostbusters," a movie that was… would be… popular when he was… would be… finishing medical school.

The responding police officer, Ned Allen, had been on the local police force for over a decade. He was well-respected, but still came across as a pompous ass in situations where he could exert power over women.

"Velma, have you been drinking again?" Officer Allen asked.

Velma Schaubelt clasped and wrung her hands as she turned her gaze downward. She did not have to answer Allen's question. Her body language told a better story than words ever could.

Officer Allen took Velma by the arm and guided her into the back seat of his patrol car. "Velma, you just sit tight right there now until I find out how the boy is." Allen's tone was patronizing and condescending.

Ned Allen walked over to the prostrate child. He asked the ambulance attendants and the milling crowd if anyone knew who the child was.

"I think it's Jimmy Simcoe," a male voice said from somewhere in the crowd.

"I think his parents live over on Hamilton," another voice said. It seemed that nobody wanted to be identified as having provided Officer Allen with any information.

"Officer Allen, can we transport the boy to Casualty?" one of the ambulance attendants asked.

"Yes… yes," Allen replied. "I will radio dispatch and ask them to contact the parents."

Turning to Stephen Wilcox, Allen commented, "Doc, it's a good thing you came along."

"Officer, I didn't do anything other than check the boy for severe injuries," Stephen Wilcox replied.

"Are you new in town?" Allen asked.

Wilcox needed to have a plausible response to that question and he paused pensively for a moment before answering, "I just came across the river from Detroit for a fancy dress party, as you can see, and I had my dates mixed up." Wilcox was anticipating that Allen would have known of of or seen other partygoers in similar attire.

"Oh, yes… And do you plan on remaining here in Amherstburg for a while, Doctor… I didn't catch your name," Allen asked.

"Wilcox. Stephen Wilcox, MD," he said.

"Officer Allen?" a female voice asked.

"Yes, Mildred?" Allen replied. His tone was as condescending as it was when he was dealing with Velma Schnaubelt.

"I would like to show Doctor Wilcox around our little town. He did, after all, seemingly save Jimmy Simcoe's life," the very attractive Mildred Krieger replied. Wilcox had already noticed she was not wearing a wedding ring.

Before Officer Allen could respond, Wilcox cut in, "Miss Krieger, I would be honored by your company. Perhaps we could find someplace for a cup of coffee – or tea, if you prefer?"

"Please call me Mildred," she replied.

"Well, I insist that you call me Stephen," he chuckled.

*　　*　　*　　*　　*

The groom, his best man, and two ushers stood waiting at the front of the church along with the pastor. They all turned towards the rear of the church as the doors opened and the organ began playing the processional piece. This particular church did not allow the playing of "Here Comes the Bride" because of its theatrical origin; instead, the organist and an accompanying trumpeter played Jeremiah Clarke's "Trumpet Voluntary."

First, the maid of honor and two bridesmaids strolled down the aisle, taking their place to the right of the

265

congregation. They wore matching pastel blue a-line gowns with cap sleeves and lace trim. Finishing the ensemble, they wore white silk elbow-length gloves.

The bride, radiant in her white gown, veil, and formal train, slowly walked down the aisle at her father's arm. Reaching the front pew of the church, she touched her mother's arm briefly and tenderly. That simple touch told the mother that her daughter was now a grown woman and ready for a life and family of her own.

Just before joining the men at the chancel rail, the bride stopped and turned to her father; she could see the tears streaming uncharacteristically down his face. It was the first time she had ever seen her father cry.

As she smiled, her father lifted the formal veil back from her face. She leaned towards him and gave him a kiss on the cheek; at the same time, he took both of her hands in his and squeezed gently. He smiled at her and whispered, "This is your day. Remember it forever."

The groom reached out to take his bride's hand from her father's and guide her into the bridal party. He chin-nodded at his soon-to-be father-in-law, thus accepting responsibility for his bride.

Smiling, he looked at her and whispered, "You are the most beautiful bride I have ever seen."

She was speechless. Overcome with the emotions of the moment – and after seeing her father in tears – she was on the verge of losing her own composure.

Reality brought everyone back to earth as the final strains of the processional music died out and the pastor began the ceremony.

"Dearly Beloved, we are gathered here today to join this man and this woman in Holy Matrimony. If there be anyone who can show cause why this marriage should not take place, let him speak now or forever hold his peace."

The bride and groom smiled at each other in the pregnant silence. Thankfully, no one spoke.

"Who gives this woman to be married to this man?"

"Her mother and I do," replied Mr. Krieger.

The initial formalities concluded, the pastor offered a short homily that surprisingly focused on Genesis 2:22-24:

"And the LORD God caused a deep sleep to fall upon Adam, and he slept: and he took one of his ribs, and closed up the flesh instead thereof;

22 And the rib, which the LORD God had taken from man, made he a woman, and brought her unto the man.

23 And Adam said, This is now bone of my bones, and flesh of my flesh: she shall be called Woman, because she was taken out of Man.

24 Therefore shall a man leave his father and his mother, and shall cleave unto his wife: and they shall be one flesh.

After his homily, the pastor coached the couple through their wedding vows.

"Do you, Stephen Wilcox, take this woman, Mildred Krieger, to be your lawfully wedded wife?"

Stephen Wilcox replied with a resounding "I do!"

Turning to the bride, the pastor asked, "Do you, Mildred Krieger, take this man, Stephen Wilcox, to be your lawfully wedded husband?"

In a voice whose strength and conviction surprised even herself, Mildred replied "I most certainly do!"

Turning back to Stephen, the pastor guided the couple through their vows. "Stephen, will you please repeat after me? I, Stephen Wilcox, take you, Mildred Krieger, to be my lawful wedded wife…"

Stephen Wilcox repeated the vows with only a slight tremor in his voice. Thanks to medical school and the war, he had remained single for nearly a decade longer than most men of his age. He was nervous and recognized that his formerly stable single life was about to change forever.

He already knew part of what the future held: the "fabulous fifties" were in full swing and "Rock Around the Clock" was about to be released by Bill Haley and the Comets. The fall of Dien Bien Phu in Vietnam was imminent and U.S. involvement there was about a decade away.

One thing that truly concerned Stephen Wilcox was his own timeline. He just had to accept that his presence in 1954 wouldn't completely alter the fabric of time.

31: A Growing Family
March, 1955

"Congratulations, Doctor Wilcox! You are the father of a healthy baby boy. Both he and your wife are doing well," the obstetrician beamed. Despite being a doctor himself, Stephen Wilcox had been relegated to the purgatory for expectant fathers – the waiting room outside of the labor and delivery suite. "If you see the charge nurse at the nursery viewing window, she will introduce you to your son."

"In less than twenty years, fathers will be expected to be in the delivery room with their wives, not pacing the floor for hours on end," Freddy thought. "Thank you, Doctor," was all that Freddy could say out loud. Less than a year ago, he couldn't imagine himself in 1955, married, and with a child.

Memories of Lizzie Pritchard in 1814 suddenly came flooding back. He realized that his relationship with her was more a matter of convenience than love and he now regretted ever proposing marriage. He was now truly in love with Mildred, who, despite being over a decade younger than himself, had just given him a son.

Hospitals in 1955 were very strict about visiting hours. Fathers, too, had to visit within the time window unless there was an emergency involving either the mother or the baby. Stephen found this odd compared to the open, round-the-clock visitation of the 1990s but had to accept it as normal. It was during late afternoon visiting hours the day after Baby Boy Wilcox was born that an administrator from the hospital came by to fill out paperwork for a birth certificate.

"Doctor and Mrs. Wilcox, congratulations on becoming parents," Mrs. White, the administrator said. "There are a few formalities we must take care of so that the birth is properly registered with the authorities." Mrs. White was all business and dressed the part: a Mamie Eisenhower hairdo, a pearl necklace, conservative high heels, and a color-coordinated ensemble was worn as if it were her uniform.

"Yes, of course," Mildred replied.

"Do you have a name for the child?" Mrs. White asked.

"We do," Stephen began, "his name will be James Kenneth Wilcox."

"James... Kenneth... Wilcox... does the middle name have one 'n' or two?" Mrs. White said as she wrote in her book.

"K-E-N-N-E-T-H, Mrs. White. Kenneth." Stephen said firmly.

"And you are James's natural parents as husband and wife?" Mrs. White asked; she was obviously judging their difference in age.

"What a dumb question," Stephen thought, *"it's not the 1960s – yet..."*

"Yes, Mrs. White, we are," Mildred said, the irritation obvious in her voice. She almost wanted to affirm that she was a virgin on her wedding night and leave it to the petty bureaucrat known as Mrs. White to prove otherwise.

"May I have your full names, please?" White asked.

"Stephen James Wilcox and Mildred Rose Krieger," Stephen answered.

"Mildred Rose Krieger *Wilcox*," Mildred corrected.

Mrs. White continued gathering the information she would need to type up the birth certificate and register the birth. Once she was finished, she told Stephen and Mildred, "I will be back at this time tomorrow with the forms you need to sign."

Stephen once again noticed the dissimilarity between 1955 and his own time. In the 1990s, Women were generally discharged from the hospital within three days of giving birth unless a Caesarean section was involved. Here, it was likely that Mildred would remain in the maternity ward for a full week before being released. It was the conventional wisdom of the day that women needed rest and assistance for the first week after giving birth; however, Wilcox knew from experience that hospitals – even ones using archaic practices like this one – were far from restful places.

Movement up and down the corridor was constant; there was no separation between the obstetrical rooms and the suite of delivery rooms. Screams of women in hard labor and the sudden squalling cries of newborns regularly pierced the silence; if more than one woman was in end-stage labor at the same time, there were even more people moving about on the floor absorbed by their assigned tasks and not caring one bit about the noise level or patients resting in nearby rooms.

Wilcox wanted to take Mildred home immediately. As a physician himself, he was quite capable of taking care of his wife postpartum. Regardless, Mildred's obstetrician remained intransigent and adamant that she should remain in the hospital for a full week. "After all," the obstetrician said condescendingly, "delivering babies and taking care of their mothers is *my* specialty. I've been doing this for over thirty years…"

After nearly losing his temper and coming to blows, Stephen Wilcox, MD, relented and agreed to leave his wife in the hospital for the full seven days.

Stephen took his wife and newborn son home on the afternoon of Mildred's seventh day after delivery. She was glad to finally be home and away from the hospital. "It was like a busy train station in there," she told Stephen, "and I could not get any rest." She was exhausted and on the verge of tears. "And… my milk has come in, too. The nurses had their own minds about when I could and couldn't nurse Jimmy. It it wasn't on their schedule, well…" Stephen knew what she was trying to tell him: her over-full breasts hurt.

"My darling," he replied, "I tried to get you released to my care on your third day, but that old coot of an obstetrician would not agree. If it had been up to me, you would have been home and resting four days ago."

At just that moment, young James decided he was hungry. "Finally! I can feed him on his schedule," Mildred beamed. I knew he would want to eat as soon as we were home. He's slept most of the day already."

Jimmy was not one of those babies that quickly developed a preference for the bottle over the breast. He latched on with vigor and Mildred smiled as the pressure in her chest – at least on the right side, anyway – was quickly relieved. Unfortunately, that also triggered her let-down reflex on the left side, and she quickly soaked through her bra and blouse. She was embarrassed.

Stephen tried to comfort her. "Mildred, my darling, take it from me as a doctor that what just happened is perfectly normal. Every nursing mother experiences it at one time or another. It is nothing to be ashamed of."

With Jimmy nursing eagerly, she smiled back at her husband, mouthing the words "Thank you!"

Mildred quickly settled into a routine with their son. It was as if they were totally in tune with each other. She would eat as soon as Jimmy was finished nursing, then drift off to sleep with him, often not waking until his next feeding.

Stephen Wilcox was the model father and helped around the house as much as he could when he wasn't seeing his own patients. The one thing that he had brought with him from 1993 was an understanding that raising children was not totally up to the mother and that children thrived when their fathers were involved. He changed diapers, learned how to do the laundry, taught himself to cook, and generally made himself indispensable to Mildred and their son. They were a team.

By now, Stephen had become a valued part of the medical community in Amherstburg. The accident involving Jimmy Simcoe had only helped cement his standing in the community. The one thing that Wilcox had to be constantly aware of was that his medical knowledge was almost forty years ahead of his current time: in 1955, there were no ultrasounds or MRIs. There was no DNA testing. There was no laparoscopic surgery. All of those things were commonplace and widely accepted in 1993. In meetings with other doctors, he often remained silent to assess the knowledge of the participants before injecting his own observations.

Before their marriage and her pregnancy, Mildred (nee Krieger) Wilcox had been employed as a secretary. She was now happily ensconced as a mother and homemaker. Going back to work never entered her mind; after all, who would take care of James? Institutional daycare was unheard of in the 1950s and Mildred's parents, despite being doting grandparents, were not inclined to give up their freedom to take care of their only grandchild – so far.

James Wilcox thrived as a toddler and preschooler. He had an aptitude for learning and grasped reading by the time he was three years old. His academic precocity would eventually get in his way and affect his behavior; he spent almost as much time in the Principal's Office or detention as he did in class. Even so, he managed to graduate from high school at sixteen and was well on his way to a doctorate before his 20th birthday. Then he met Jacqui Wilcox…

32: Meanwhile, Back in 1814…
Vicinity of Amherstburg, Spring-Summer, 1814

The Potawatomi band was as agriculturally proficient as it was in hunting and fishing. Their knowledge made their health and survival a near certainty. The only unpredictable variable was the possibility of diseases from the rapidly advancing white population. It was smallpox that was the most feared by Natives, regardless of their tribal ancestry and affiliation.

Smallpox was dreaded as much for its disfiguring characteristics as it was for its mortality. The Potawatomi, like most Native American bands, took great pride in personal appearance: body scars were considered badges of honor if they came from warfare or encounters with wild beasts. Conversely, scars from intangible causes like viruses were punishments delivered from the spirit world for some sort of infraction. Even Christian bands like White Moon's still carried the old beliefs as part of their heritage.

I was not expecting that our visit to Fort Shelby a few weeks earlier would put us in contact with a cluster of individuals who were active carriers of the smallpox virus. That proximity made me the 1814 equivalent of an asymptomatic "patient zero" outside of Fort Shelby. Sure, I had been vaccinated in my own time – but what about the Potawatomi village? I did not want to be the one who infected them with the dreaded disease.

Fortunately, White Moon and her family remained free of smallpox, and I wondered if they had some sort of natural immunity. Because we were well outside the incubation period for the virus after returning from Fort Shelby, I had no trepidation about discussing the matter with White Moon.

"White Moon, do you know what smallpox is?" I asked one evening as we were preparing for our dinner.

"Yes, I do. I have seen American and British soldiers infected with the disease. Many of them die, and the ones who live are scarred for life," she answered.

"Can you explain why your village does not get infected?" My curiosity was piqued.

"When my father was here two years ago before the trapping season, he insisted on poking needles in our…" she paused and pointed to her gluteus maximus, "after dipping them in some powder that he had in a dark green bottle. I asked him to explain what he was doing, and he told me that it was to prevent smallpox."

I had to laugh at her false modesty as she pointed to her wonderful shapely backside. I knew that variolation, like Jenner's vaccination, was usually administered in a patient's arm. "Why did your father insist on doing it back there?" I asked.

"He understood our pride and desire not to be scarred unless it was from a battle wound or a wild animal. The way he did it made sure that the scar would remain hidden," she explained.

"What did Grandmother She-Eagle say about that?" I asked.

"She was unsure at first, but after my father explained that he had lived in a smallpox infected camp for many months and never caught the disease – because he had poked the needles in himself," White Moon explained.

"White Moon, when Dr. Wilcox and I went to Fort Shelby, we may have been exposed to smallpox. There were several soldiers who were obviously recovering. We shot and killed two of them when they tried to raid our campsite on the riverbank."

White Moon's expression told me that she was greatly concerned by our violent and deadly encounter with the infected men.

"Marcus, you could have been killed!" she exclaimed.

"It's not the first time I have been exposed to danger like that. Back in my time, well… let's just agree that I had been in similar situations before," I said. I did not want to delve too deep into the details of my deployments to hostile areas, nor any of the intricacies of 20th Century wars and warfare.

For the rest of the evening, there was a tense silence between us. She knew that we had only done what was necessary.

As we lay under our light blankets that evening trying to drift off to sleep through the tension, White Moon suddenly squealed. It was a high-pitched squeal of delight. I rolled over to see what she was so happy about.

"Marcus, put your hand here…" White Moon said, taking my hand in hers and guiding it towards her belly. "Can you feel that?" she asked.

"Yes, my darling, I can… Is that our baby?" I asked.

"Well, it certainly isn't a squirrel," she giggled.

It was the first time she had been able to feel the baby move on the outside of her belly. Up to now, it had only been a sensation of movement inside her. She wanted to run to She-Eagle's lodge and tell her the good news as well.

As White Moon started to stand, I moved more quickly to prevent her from rising. I took her in my arms and kissed her deeply. It was definitely one of those "make-up kisses" I had seen in the movies and I knew exactly what would follow the kiss; it was definitely a fade-to-black moment.

The next morning, I decided to find out more about White Moon's father. I already knew he was white and most likely British or American, but not much else. How could he have been aware of variolation and the technique required to administer it? I knew from my coursework that immunity from smallpox infection was possible long before the vaccine itself had been invented. In fact, variolation might even have predated the Christian era.

"White Moon, did any of you get sick after your father scratched your backsides with the powder?" I asked.

"Some of us did, but not all. The ones that got sick were just feverish and did not develop the ugly sores all over their bodies," White Moon explained.

"The men we saw at Fort Shelby had obviously not been vaccinated. They were grossly disfigured from the pox, but I don't know if they would have died from the infection," I observed.

"Marcus, it is still fortunate that you were not killed in the ambush. That would have been unbearable."

"Can you tell me more about your father, White Moon?" I asked. "He seems to have been a smart man."

"IS a smart man," she interjected. He is still alive and wanders the forests during the winter, trapping beaver and other animals for their fur. We never know when he will be here on his way to sell his furs in Detroit," she said with a wistful look in her eye, "and the rest of the year, he guides settlers heading west from Virginia down the Ohio River on barges. We see him even less in the growing season than we do in the winter."

"Will he be offended that you have taken an American man, a white American man, as your husband?" I asked. If her father was the typical rough-and-tumble frontiersman with traditional values, I might be in big trouble.

"He loves my mother and it would be hippo… hippo… hypocritical for him to take offense to my choice of husband," White Moon assured me.

"Let's hope I don't have to wait too long to find out," I teased.

"It is nearly time for planting and Father should be spending a few weeks with us waiting for the floodwaters on the Ohio River to subside. It is more dangerous if he goes too early in the season," White Moon said with a smile.

"Isn't the Ohio River a long distance away?" I asked.

"He goes south to the Miami River and takes a canoe to where it meets the Ohio," White Moon explained. "He works his way down the river to the Mississippi and, when snow flies, traps his way back north. I think your people would call him a nomad, or maybe even a hermit."

"I can't wait to be properly introduced," I said.

With White Moon's explanation, I now knew more about her father. I was, however, still puzzled about her mother, who I apparently had never met. White Moon rarely spoke of her mother – at least not in the same way a white woman would, with love and wistful fond memories. Affirming that her father loved her mother was one of those rare occasions. I decided to press the issue.

"White Moon, why do you never speak of your mother?" I asked as we were cleaning up the remains of our breakfast.

"My mother? What do you mean, Marcus? You have spoken to her many times," White Moon answered..

"My darling, I don't understand."

"In our custom, once a woman is of a certain age, she is called "Grandmother. It doesn't matter if she has grandchildren or not. It is a sign of respect for her age and wisdom. We give her that title when her youngest child reaches adulthood."

"Wait… are you telling me that Grandmother She-Eagle is really your mother?" I was shocked as I realized the truth.

"Yes, Marcus, you are correct. Grandmother She-Eagle bore me," White Moon explained.

I found the revelation somewhat hard to get used to. "Why did you not tell me this earlier, even before we were married?" I asked. The friction between us was building and had every chance of erupting into one of our infrequent, but very vocal, disagreements.

"Marcus, if you will recall, just getting my village to accept you as my husband was no small task. It was simpler to just call her 'Grandmother' and not confuse you with more information about our culture," White Moon answered. "There just wasn't enough time to explain it all to you."

"I understand, my darling, but we've been married for several months now, and I should have known this from the start," I said with obvious displeasure in my voice. "I'm going for a walk." I picked up my pistol and cartridge pouch as I walked out the door. With the fort no longer posting guards overnight, it was prudent to be armed.

Calmly, I left of our quarters and strode out to the perimeter of Fort Malden. It was a quiet, still, moonlight night and the only sounds to be heard were the occasional howls of a pack of coyotes, the hooting of barred owls, and the repetitive shrill of whippoorwills. The sounds of these creatures were a very relaxing natural symphony and I quickly forgot that I was… no, not angry… frustrated with White Moon's withholding of information that I should have been provided with much earlier in our relationship.

Reaching the riverbank to the west of Fort Malden, I sat down on a log and was mesmerized by the reflection of the moon on the barely rippling water. I sat there for a few contemplative minutes that were disturbed by the sounds of a large creature making its way through the brush to the south of where I was sitting. We had recently seen evidence of both black bears and wolves transiting the area, and I did not want to become the next meal of either species.

With my senses on high alert, I eased my pistol from my waist sash and turned to face the direction of the sound's origin. I hoped it was not a pack of wolves, as I would not stand a chance against a coordinated attack. The initial report from the pistol would temporarily frighten them, but they would quickly regroup – perhaps before I could reload for a second shot.

The thought then entered my mind that it might be a human being who had adapted their movements to mimic a large animal. I had learned long ago that a biped human moving through dried leaves and scrub brush made unique sounds, while a quadruped was more subtle. In either case, I would make sure my first shot was well-aimed. The situation was tense and my heart felt as if it were going to explode.

"You there, on the riverbank!" a voice called out, "I know you are armed and ready to fire. I mean you no harm and will show myself presently," the voice said firmly.

There was something very familiar about that voice. I had heard it before but couldn't place it. The voice had a no-nonsense tone of authority. I hesitated before responding to allow my brain a chance to process the familiarity.

After what seemed like an eternity, I was ready to respond. "Show yourself, stranger, with your weapons remaining in your belt and your hands high!"

"As you wish," came the reply.

33: A Strange Reunion
Spring-Summer, 1814

I instantly recognized the human form coming towards me in the light of a nearly full moon. The gait and mannerisms were unmistakable despite the long hair and beard. It was none other than Sean Hagerty!

"Is that you, Sean?" I asked incredulously. Deciding I needed to be certain, I offered up one of the challenge-reply passphrases from one of our deployments: "Captain Kangaroo, is that you?"

"More importantly, is that *you*, Marcus?" came the reply, followed by the appropriate response: "It's Mister Green Jeans with the beans."

"Yes, my old friend, it is you!" I responded as I stood up and ran towards my friend. *Could I be dreaming?* I thought to myself. *Did the argument with White Moon take over my thoughts and make me subconsciously wish I were somewhere else?*

With the formalities of a man-hug and a firm handshake behind us, we began a rapid-fire debrief of each other's escapades and time travels.

"How did you get here?" Sean asked.

"It was on Commemoration Day when I was a re-enactor. The stack of cannonballs was mathematically significant: a seven-by-seven square pyramid totaling 204 spheres. A surveyor explained the mathematical concepts to me here… in 1813, just after the Battle of Lake Erie, when I was put in command of the hospital here at Fort Malden by none other than Oliver Hazard Perry himself!"

"We found your dogtags in the mud at the South Bass Island Marina," Sean explained, "which was the likely site of the wharf for Perry's Lake Erie naval base. I just knew you had not simply vanished into the depths of the lake like the local authorities believed. It all makes sense now."

"Makes sense? What do you mean, Sean?"

"I will tell you more about my own travels in a few minutes, but I can tell you with certainty that anything from the future that would have been out of place in the past is left behind. People making the jump from one time to another often reach their destination naked because their clothes from the future would have been out of place. I assume that you arrived in 1813 fully clothed?"

"Yes, Sean, as a matter of fact, I was fully clothed," I answered, "and was immediately set upon by an officer who

was so absorbed in his own perceived importance that he was
ready to have me flogged for drunkenness. It was probably
lucky for me that I had been dressed for the re-enactment in
a proper Navy work uniform; I shudder to think what would
have happened to me if that strutting martinet of an officer
had come across me in my birthday suit."

"He probably would have thought you were Jewish, if
you know what I mean," Sean said with a chuckle.

"Oh, yeah… right… they didn't routinely do *that* to boy
babies in the 18th Century, did they?" I replied, trying to
stifle a laugh.

"Are you going to offer me a place to stay for the night?"
Sean asked. "With so much to talk about, I doubt either of us
will be getting much sleep."

"You don't even need to ask. My quarters are on the other
side of the fort, or what's left of it, anyway. My wife…"

Sean interrupted, "Your wife? After all these years as a
single man? You time-hop and suddenly decide to settle
down?"

"Sean, she's pregnant, but that's not why we got married.
We fell in love." I paused to choose my next words carefully.
"She's a Native, from the Potawatomi band across the river.

We spend about half of our time in her village, as I have technically resigned my brevet commission. I'm just awaiting confirmation from Commodore Perry and General Harrison that my resignation has been accepted. It's been months since I sent the letter with a courier… Anyway… she chose me, as is the custom of her village, to be her husband and I have been accepted into her family as one of their own."

"Marcus, I can't wait to meet her. She sounds like a good woman. She'd have to be good to take in the likes of you!" Sean said as he slapped me firmly on the back. "Let's go."

It seemed almost as if we had been transported across Fort Malden without even touching the ground. Reaching the door to my quarters, I opened it and stepped inside. "White Moon, my darling…"

Seeing Sean Hagerty coming in behind me, she looked like she had seen a ghost and was briefly unsteady on her feet.

"Papa!" White Moon screamed, "you're home!'

Now I was thoroughly confused. Not only was my best friend a time traveler like me, but also apparently my father-in-law as well. I wanted answers and I wanted them *now*. I was totally taken aback by my wife's greeting to my best friend – and now apparently my father-in-law as well.

"Which one of you is going to explain this all to me?"

White Moon spoke first, feigning ignorance of anything. "Papa just appears when the time is right for us to plant," she explained.

"It's complicated, Marcus," Sean said as he slowly shook his head from side to side. "When you left 2017 and the re-enactment on South Bass Island, I had no idea you had traveled through time – nor was I even aware that time travel was possible. It took some doing and multiple hops through time before I finally got here to 1814, unsure if I would ever find you alive."

"Multiple hops? How did you figure that out?"

"It took some doing and a lot of research, but I determined that there were magical powers in square pyramids made from stacked spherical objects. I also found a connection to ancient Greece and a goddess called Hecate," Sean explained, "the math was a bit of a challenge, but I worked it out in the end – and we are not the only ones involved with South Bass Island to have made jumps through time. Do you remember the owners of that B & B where we stayed while we were doing the salvage dives?"

"Of course," I replied, "James and Jacqui Wilcox, but what do they have to do with any of this?"

"Well… making a long story short," Sean said with a sigh, "I accidentally stumbled across a time portal that took me back to 1748. That wasn't so bad, at least not until I saw Jacqui Wilcox in the same Potawatomi village that White Moon comes from. I high tailed it out of there before Jacqui saw me."

"Sean, that's unbelievable. What gave you access to the time portal?" I asked.

"At first, it was Hecate's Wheel, like I told you. I went back 270 years from 2018," Hagerty explained, "but the rest I will have to tell you privately." Hagerty gave a chin thrust towards his daughter, White Moon, with that last statement, indicating that he wanted to tell me something that was not suitable for her ears, daughter/wife or not. She had not seen his gesture and was none the wiser as she understood that there were some things that were truly "men's business," even in Potawatomi culture.

Once we were outside, Sean seemed quite agitated. I was curious how he managed to track me down to 1814. If he was indeed White Moon's biological father, he would have had to jump to the 1790s to marry She-Eagle. The possibilities and realities were almost too confusing to contemplate.

"Marcus, I know it seems odd to you for me to show up literally on your doorstep. It was an educated guess on my part, informed by the research James Wilcox had done into his own family tree," Sean explained.

"What exactly did you learn from Wilcox, Sean?" I asked.

"Well… it wasn't exactly from Wilcox," Sean said as he stepped closer and dropped his voice to a whisper, "jt was from his notes, the ones that were posted all over his home office like a police investigation's murder board."

"Sean, I don't quite understand. Can you tell me a little more?" I asked.

"He called me in the middle of the winter wondering if I had seen his wife. You remember her, don't you?" he teased.

"I most certainly do. I caught her staring at my body when I was changing into the dive suit before we started the salvage operation," I said with a wink.

Sean continued, "Sometime after you disappeared, she did as well. James was frantic, thinking she might have run off with you, even though your disappearance preceded hers by several months. I tried to explain to Wilcox that there was no way the two disappearances could be related. He didn't want to believe me and even went so far as to accuse me of complicity."

"Wow, that's a stretch," I noted. "I had no interest in that woman whatsoever."

"I had to settle the matter once and for all," Sean said, "and needed to get to South Bass Island for an in-person meeting. The only way out to the island was by snowmobile – as long as the Lake Erie ice was sold and smooth enough. The problem I had was that a traditional snowmobile makes quite a bit of noise and I really wanted to get to the island without drawing a lot of attention to myself."

I looked at him quizzically. "So, what did you do?" I asked.

"One of my Canadian associates had recently developed a prototype electric snowmobile and wanted me to check it out before they took it to market. He was pretty certain it would have enough range to make it to South Bass Island and back again without recharging. It was only a little more than a six-mile round trip. Aside from the tread noise on the ice, it would have been nearly silent."

Sean continued, "I made the trip just before nightfall, somehow managing to avoid detection by the gossips who stayed on the island through the winter. After securing my machine, I hoofed it to the B & B. Strangely, the kitchen door was not latched. That told me something was not quite right."

"Did you go inside?" I asked.

"Yes… I pushed the door open slowly with my gloved hand. If anything was amiss, I did not want to leave any traceable fingerprints; remember, ours are on file with the Feds, as is our DNA… Anyway, once I got into the B & B, there was no one on the ground floor at all. I called out several times in a loud whisper, 'Jacqui? James? Are you here?' and got no reply. That was when I noticed that the entire B & B was quite cold."

"That's odd," I said, "Jacqui was a fastidious innkeeper and certainly would not have allowed the place to go unmaintained through the winter."

"I decided that there might be some foul play involved, so I took my Glock out of my waist pack and carefully began an indoor search. It sure would have been nice for someone to have my six as I moved through the house. It was so quiet that I could hear the rats scurrying and gnawing within the walls. It was pretty disgusting," said Sean. "I got about halfway up the stairs to the second floor when a board creaked under my feet. If anyone had been home, that would have given me away and I froze, Glock in the ready position, I expected someone to reveal themselves. Nothing happened."

I was now wondering if Sean had become unwittingly involved in some sort of foul play beyond the disappearance of Jacqui Wilcox. His detailed story sounded almost as if he were trying to provide himself with an alibi, should one be necessary. I needed more details and wanted to believe that everything he was doing (or was it "had done"? or even "would do"?) on South Bass Island that cold winter evening was above board. Ultimately, I had to trust his loyalty to our Special Warfare Operator's Code of Conduct and that he would provide me with truthful information.

Sean continued, "At the top of the stairs, I walked down the hallway to the partially open door, guessing that I would find James Wilcox up to his ears in sticky notes and genealogical charts. I entered the room and secured my weapon in my waist pack. Seeing James, it looked as if he was asleep at his desk, head resting on forearms. 'James,' I called out three times, hoping to rouse him from his apparent slumber."

Sean's presentation was sounding more and more like a post-mission debrief. He was giving me all the relevant details without any embellishment, sticking to just the facts, where other military members not bound by our Code would have given hyperbolic descriptions. I knew I could trust my old friend.

Hagerty continued, "When James did not rouse from my calls, I moved closer and checked his carotid pulse. There was none, and his skin was cold to the touch. James Wilcox was dead and had probably been for quite some time."

"Did you report what you found to the authorities?" I asked.

"No, I did not," he answered. "I assumed that there was already a Missing Person's Report on Jacqui and certainly did not want to get hauled in for questioning as to her whereabouts. I knew where… when… she was, aid the police would not have believed it."

34: A Long Night
Summer, 1814

Before I realized it, dawn was breaking to the east. Sean and I had been up all night talking about his exploits as a time traveler. He had made multiple jumps in time, where I had only made one, from 2017 to 1813. Sean, on the other hand, had seen 1814, 1724, 1744, 1658, and 1969 – and not necessarily in that order.

What was the most interesting was Sean's connection to the Potawatomi band that had accepted me as their own after marrying White Moon. It turned out that Sean likely was White Moon's great-great grandfather as well as her biological father. It was a confusing story.

After White Moon had explained to me that "Grandmother" She-Eagle was really her mother, I pressed her for more details about her lineage. As it was nearly all oral history and legend handed down through the generations, I had to be circumspect in my acceptance of her story. Regardless, it turned out that the only intersection between her story and that of Sean Hagerty's was a reference to a young Potawatomi woman named Chipmunk, sometime before the French and Indian War. Chipmunk was apparently White Moon's great-grandmother.

Hagerty explained to me that in his earlier visits to the Potawatomi village, the area was under French influence. During this time, the Potawatomi understood his name to be "Jean" rather than Sean – as we would say in military radio jargon, "good garbles" for each other. I was completely baffled as to how he had managed to maintain the ruse of assimilation into the societies of each period he visited.

"What was it like for you to travel in time, Sean?" I asked.

"Each time was different," he answered. "Sometimes, I would see history flashing before my eyes. Other times, it was as if I was instantly transported from one time to the next."

"That matches my own experience jumping from 2018 to 1813," I observed. "Like I said before, it was as if I had fallen asleep and suddenly awoke in the middle of preparations for the Battle of Lake Erie. I was even accused of being drunk on duty by an officer because I could not tell him what year it was. From there, I was pressed into service on Perry's flagship, the *USS Lawrence*."

"You already know about the tree carving near Detroit – in what will become Witherell Woods within Palmer Park. It still exists in 2018 and I believe it is where Jacqui Wilcox made her jump to 1748. The math all works out," Hagerty explained.

"Did you ever run across a Lizzie… Elizabeth Pritchard in your travels, Sean?" I asked.

"I don't think so," he answered. "Any idea of what year she ended up in?"

"Based on your observations, it likely would have been 1634," I said. "She was Dr. Stephen Wilcox's erstwhile fiancée and disappeared the night he was supposed to jump forward to 1994. Thanks to some subterfuge on his part, she made the jump – backwards, I think – instead of him. He panicked at the last minute."

"There is a Potawatomi legend about a naked white woman, if you could call her that, appearing magically out of thin air near the carving, but the year is not certain," Sean noted, "and she was killed on the spot. The legend said the poor woman was so ugly and deformed that she could be nothing other than a witch. The Potawatomi back then, before their conversion to Christianity by French missionaries, were a superstitious bunch."

"Hmm… Sounds like the Salem Witch Trials in Massachusetts about sixty years later. I had wondered if someone who was forced into time travel like she was would have arrived in their new time as a whole person. I think you just answered that question for me, Sean," I acknowledged.

There was a pause in our discussion when I sensed that White Moon was now awake and taking care of her morning ablutions. I heard the door to our quarters open and saw her shuffling her way to the privy. When she saw Sean – her father – and me sitting on a log, she smiled and waved. "*If she only knew*," I thought to myself.

On her way back from the privy, White Moon came closer to us and asked if we would like some breakfast. Our response was enthusiastic. It had been a long night and we were famished.

"Father… Marcus…" she said, "I will call for you when breakfast is ready."

When she was out of hearing range, I chuckled, "Sean, I just can't get used to the idea that you are her father."

"Nor can I get my head around the fact that you are her husband, Marcus."

I decided to change the subject while we waited for White Moon to call us in for breakfast.

'Sean, earlier, you mentioned that your time travels allowed you to see some events in history as you passed through on your way to your next destination. What were some of the things you saw?" I asked.

"The longest span of time that I jumped was from 2018 to 1658. That jump was enabled by the tree carving in Palmer Park. It was weird," Hagerty said as his voice trailed off to a near-whisper.

"What do you mean, 'weird'?" I asked.

"I saw snippets from nearly all of the wars of the 20th Century. Vietnam, Korea, World War II, World War I... It was always obvious which war I was passing through. It was more of an experience than a connection to a place or battle. I think I was being shown how warfare had evolved over time, but in reverse order."

Hagerty continued, "It was surreal. I suddenly knew everything there was to know about each of those wars, even though I had not studied them in any depth beyond the battles they used for tactical examples in our training. Right now, I wouldn't be able to recall any significant facts about them – but I believe if you ask the right questions, I will be able to give you answers that are excruciatingly detailed."

"What happened with the 19th Century?" I asked.

"Again, each of the United States' wars came into sharp focus: the Spanish-American War, the long and sordid string of the American Indian Wars, the Civil War, the Mexican American War, the War of 1812 – "

I interrupted, "Sean, I get the point. It's been a long night, and we still have so much to discuss. I suggest that we take advantage of White Moon's breakfast, get some sleep, and continue this discussion when we are both well-rested." I paused for a moment before asking Sean, "Does White Moon know about your time travels?"

"She does not, my old friend. Does she know about yours?" Hagerty asked.

"Yes. She explained the legend to me," I replied, "and we facilitated the time travel of our former military physician to 1954. That was when I confirmed the relationship between the tree carving and a symbol that was on the final cannonball I stacked from our 2017 salvage dives. Doctor Wilcox –"

Sean interrupted, "Was that by chance a Doctor Stephen Wilcox?"

"Yes, it was," I answered, furrowing my brow. "Is that important?"

"Well… it turns out that a Doctor Stephen Wilcox is – or will be – James Wilcox's father – you know… the one from the Bed and Breakfast on South Bass Island and now the dead guy," Sean explained.

I had so many questions that needed… demanded… answers. Our conversation, however was interrupted by White Moon opening the door to our quarters and announcing that breakfast – and coffee – were ready. The aromas of coffee brewing, venison sausage cooking and biscuits baking made both of our mouths water. We double-timed it to the threshold, where White Moon insisted that we both remove our boots and wash in the kitchen basin before sitting at the table. We complied without question.

At the breakfast table, after saying a prayer, White Moon engaged her father in small talk about the upcoming planting season and her growing belly.

"When do you expect the baby to be born?" he asked.

"Sometime before the harvest, I think," she answered, gently rubbing her belly.

"I will try to be here when your time comes," Sean said. "There is no way I would miss the birth of my first grandson."

"Father, have you already been to the village and visited Grandmother She-Eagle?" White Moon asked.

"Of course I have, my daughter. Do you think I would have passed her by after being gone for far too long? I've been back for several days already, and we rarely left her lodge," he said with a wink. "It was your mother who told me where to find you."

She blushed, knowing exactly what he meant. She was certainly no longer a child.

35: What Next?
Summer of 1814

The spring planting was complete. This marked the end of Sean's stay with us in this time period. He had so far managed to maintain his ruse that his presence was temporary and that he needed to head south to take on clients needing Ohio River guides. In the weeks since his arrival, he had confirmed what White Moon, She-Eagle, and the rest of the Potawatomi allegedly believed about his intermittent presence. He wanted it to stay that way. Their legends associated with previous time travelers always seemed to have destructive endings.

While Hagerty was with us, he also intimated that when he jumped backwards in time (which had happened more often than jumping ahead), his knowledge of what would be the future was nothing more than a reference point. His mind was always wiped of any tangible forward-looking knowledge. It seemed that whatever… whoever… was enabling his time hopping did not want him to influence the past based on his knowledge of the future. It appeared that this did not apply to me, as I had full recollection of my time in the future. Perhaps it was because Sean's time travels were of his own volition, whereas mine was an unintended outcome of a series of related actions. That was my theory, anyway.

There was one thing that baffled me: I had full recollection of future events, but whenever I tried to convey those memories to someone who was not a fellow traveler, I became tongue-tied and unable to speak. It was as if an unseen force was intervening to suppress my ability to share that future knowledge.

Between She-Eagle and White Moon, Sean was well-provisioned for his trek to the Ohio River. He was laden with smoked venison and elk, along with some pemmican for emergency use. The two women had also made sure that he had plenty of hardtack. The preserved dietary offerings of the period were, in my opinion, not as palatable as fresh food cooked over a campfire. Regardless, Sean Hagerty would not starve.

On our penultimate night together before he took his leave to spend the night with She-Eagle, Sean took me aside and told me more about his jumps through time. The things that he had seen and experienced defied all imagination. What was the most interesting to me, though, was that he had seen Jacqui Wilcox in 1748 as she entered the Potawatomi village with Chipmunk, his other daughter from another time. Somehow, he managed to avoid being seen. He told me that he immediately went back to the tree carving and jumped ninety years backwards in time, to 1658.

"It was bizarre," Sean recalled, "and because it happened in the past, relative to right now, of course, that I have full memory of what I had seen and done. Somehow, I was transported to a crypt beneath a church in New Haven, Connecticut. I could hear the sounds of a wedding ceremony, when all of a sudden, pandemonium broke loose. I climbed a hidden staircase – more of a ladder, really – and realized I was in a chamber built into the altar. I quietly slid the access panel open and, seeing there was no one watching that side of the altar, slid out into the chancel, and blended into the crowd."

"Why New Haven?" I asked.

"I don't know. I had never been there before and had no connection to that city," Sean answered, "and I have not even tried to figure it out. It was the only time I had ever been to New England."

"What else can you tell me, Sean?" I asked.

"Well, it seems that the wedding was interrupted by the groom dropping dead in his tracks and the bride riding off with a small group of Natives. It was easy to follow them to their village," said Sean. "Eventually, I tracked them to another tree carving like the one here in Witherell Woods."

Sean went on for just under an hour telling me about that time and the mob scene that was quelled only by the persistence of the town preacher. He certainly had had his share of adventures since the 2017 diving operations. I was more than a little but jealous.

Until now, my entire adult life had been along a single timeline with the certainty of planning and executing to accomplish specific objectives. Now, everything was in a state of flux and I could see no clear path to the final objective. Heck, at this point, I didn't even know what that final objective should be. Was it my return to 2018? Was it remaining here in 1814 with White Moon and our child? Did I need to prepare her for a jump forward to my time, asking her to leave her family and traditions behind? It was all as clear as mud.

I decided that my best approach to dealing with all of this uncertainty was to wait until Sean Hagerty had departed for his next adventure – which did not involve guiding settlers down the Ohio River to the Mississippi, as he had so expertly convinced She-Eagle and White Moon. He was, I observed, a poster child for offensive psychological warfare.

Though he was intentionally misleading the two Potawatomi women, I believe he truly loved them both. That was the only logical explanation I could come up with for his repeated returns to this time period. With the conditions of the 19th Century being so unpredictable, he could have just as easily *not* returned and perhaps faked a letter describing his demise, enabling him to vanish from their lives. There were no real-time fact checkers in 1814…

At sunset on the day of Sean's planned departure, we went to the tree carving in Witherell Woods. We made sure that White Moon, She-Eagle and Running Deer were indisposed and unlikely to follow us to the glyph.

I had almost forgotten about Running Deer, White Moon's older brother. Was he Sean's son, or did She-Eagle have a husband before Sean? It was another little detail I had to find out.

We were finally in the clearing near the tree carving. I knew our remaining time together would be short, so I decided to cut to the chase and ask the question.

"Sean, do you know Running Deer, White Moon's brother?" I asked.

"Yes, Marcus, I do. He is my son, and I am proud of the man, warrior, and provider he has become," Hagerty answered. "He is a man of his own now, and as long as he supports his mother and sister, I have no say in his comings and goings."

"Where... when... do you plan to go next?" I asked Hagerty as we slowly approached the carving.

"I think I should go forward in time, maybe to 1904. That's ninety years in the future and before World War I," he explained. "I know so little about that time that I thought it would be interesting to visit."

"Now that you have the time pinned down, what about the location?" I asked.

"I think right here near Detroit would be fine. There's always the Sauk Trail that will take me west and around the southern end of Lake Michigan if I want to do a little exploring," Sean said with a wink and a smile.

"What if you come back here to make another jump in time and the tree carving is gone?" The concern in my voice was obvious.

"Marcus, you haven't been very observant, have you? Did you even notice that the tree carving has always appeared to be fresh and that the wood has not aged? You just flunked your field evaluation, my boy," Hagerty teased.

"Now that you mention it, Sean, I do see that the carving looks to be as fresh as the day it was done. She-Eagle told me the legend of the glyph and that it enabled people to visit from another time. I didn't connect the dots to her suggestion that it had been here for many generations,"

"Marcus, it's time," Sean said as he extended his hand.

After a firm handshake and man hug, we separated and I let Sean Hagerty go to the glyph. Placing his right hand at top dead center and his left palm firmly in the center of the circle, he slowly traced through ninety degrees of arc and stopped. He looked at me over his shoulder and smiled. In a blue flash, he was gone. It seemed as if he had been completely absorbed into the circle carving and the tree.

As with Stephen Wilcox's departure, I was thrown several feet away from the tree by the pressure wave. Still slightly dazed when I stood up, I stumbled drunkenly towards the path back to the Potawatomi village, where I was to meet White Moon and spend the night in our lodge. It usually was not safe to travel through the woods after sunset, but I was now alone. Aside from my single loaded pistol and razor-sharp hunting knife, I was not prepared to spend the night sleeping rough. I had no choice but to return to the village.

White Moon was waiting for me when I arrived about an hour later. She had seen the blue flash and wanted to know where I was when it happened. I paused for a moment before answering her.

"White Moon, I don't know what you might have seen. It could have been lightning," I teased, knowing that the sky had been crystal-clear and that there were no thunderstorms anywhere nearby.

"It was the same flash we saw when Stephen Wilcox left us for another time," she said sternly, "and if you will remember, I was there, too. He just didn't leave from the tree carving."

Hanging my head sheepishly, I did my best to deflect and delay my response. She knew more about the time travelers passing through this area than she was telling me, and I did not want to anger her any further than I already had. Her moods had been all over the place lately, and the last thing I wanted was to have a tearful pregnant wife on my hands when we were away from the privacy we enjoyed on Fort Malden. Potawatomi women generally hid their emotions well, but not when they were pregnant.

"White Moon, we need to discuss our future. You seem to know more about people coming and going from another time than you are telling me," I said succinctly.

"Husband, you are correct. The story I told you about my father was nothing more than what he had been telling our village since I was old enough to remember. When I was given a woman's wisdom, I realized that he was not entirely truthful in his stories and guessed that he, too, was probably a traveler," she explained. "I know he has been back and forth many times since I was a little girl."

"If we could, would you like to go to the future with me?" I asked.

"I would like nothing better for us and our child," she said, beaming.

"The year I left was 2017, over two hundred years in the future. Things are… will be… so much different then and I cannot even begin to share with you how amazing the world will be."

"Will it be better for our child to be born then, and not here in the Year of Our Lord 1814?" she asked. "So many babies die young, both white and Potawatomi."

"Yes, my darling, things are better in the future for both mother and baby. For some reason, I can't remember the many ways things are better. You will just have to accept my word that they are."

36: Ad Futurum

(To the Future)

Summer, 1814

With Sean now gone from 1814, White Moon and I could focus on our next steps. She had agreed that it would be best for us to go forward in time but was conflicted about leaving her family and especially her mother, She-Eagle, behind. I knew intuitively that it was possible for two people to jump across time together, but I had no idea if groups of three or more would confuse the tree circle portals. I did not want to be the one to try; Sean's story of what had likely happened to Lizzie Pritchard was enough to stop those contemplations dead in their tracks.

"Marcus," White Moon crooned over breakfast the morning after Sean had left, "we probably should go sooner than later… do you think we could go tonight?"

"We won't be able to use the tree carving like your father did," I explained, "it is not as precise as the musket ball stack we used for Stephen Wilcox. I think I still have every one of those musket balls – and the one we had engraved in Amherstburg with the glyph… symbol… from the tree. I think all we have to do is keep our hands together as we put the final ball on top of the pyramid."

"Do you think we can take anything with us?" she asked.

"I would imagine only what we can affix to our bodies. You know, clothes, a few provisions… that sort of thing," I said with a pensive nod. "We also need to discuss your name in the future. Perhaps 'Luna,' which means 'moon' in Latin?" I suggested.

White Moon beamed as she replied, "Luna is a wonderful name, and I shall accept it as my own in our future, but first I must tell Grandmother She-Eagle that we are leaving. She will be upset but will understand. She is wise," White Moon said as a tear welled up in her eye to replace her previous look of happiness.

"Tonight it is," I said calmly in agreement, taking her hand tenderly into mine before drawing her close for a passionate kiss.

*　*　*　*　*

As we prepared to take our leave of Fort Malden for the final time and repair to the Potawatomi village, a lone rider approached from the east. He was in a somewhat tattered American military uniform. Judging from the leather pouches attached to his saddle, I assumed he was a courier of some kind. He reined in his horse near the water trough and hitching post just inside the perimeter of the fort.

Dismounting, the rider stood to attention and saluted even though I was not in uniform. "Sir, Private Jenkins with a dispatch for Lieutenant Marcus Harris, United States Navy. Can you tell me his whereabouts?"

I returned his salute and replied, "Stand at ease, Jenkins. I am Lieutenant Harris. Please give me the dispatch."

"Of course, sir," he replied as we dropped our salutes at the same time.

The dispatch was rolled, sealed with wax, and tied with a blue ribbon. I carefully opened it and unrolled the thick parchment to read its contents with White Moon at my side.

"Lieutenant Harris," the letter began as I read aloud, "It is with deepest respect and admiration that I accept your resignation from service as a commissioned officer in the United States Navy, effective upon receipt of this letter. Signed, Commodore Oliver Hazard Perry, Great Lakes Fleet." It was dated nearly six months earlier; having that letter finally in hand was more important than determining the cause of the inordinate delay.

White Moon's face lit up in happiness. "Marcus, does that mean we… you… are finally free to do what you please?"

I took her in my arms and kissed her deeply. "We could leave Fort Malden tonight, if that's what you want."

A few hours later, after dinner, we counted the musket balls, took our meager belongings in hand, climbed into our canoe, and headed for the Potawatomi village on the other side of the river. Mid-stream, I was suddenly filled with dread and foreboding. I stopped paddling and let the canoe drift a little to the south as I collected my thoughts.

As I analyzed what was happening in my mind, things suddenly became crystal clear: within the next twenty-five years, nearly all of the Natives in this part of the Michigan Territory would be driven from their land and sent to reservations in the Kansas and Oklahoma Territories. Something or someone had to intervene.

"White Moon, I think we need to delay our departure for a few days," I said as my mind cleared of the vision. "There is something bad that will be happening to your people unless we can figure out a way to stop it," I explained to her.

"You've had a vision of the future, haven't you?" White Moon asked.

"Yes, my darling, I have. A man named Andrew Jackson will become President of the United States in a few years and try to drive the Potawatomi west and out of the Michigan Territory. In my vision, I saw a man named Leopold Pokagon. He is the key to the Potawatomi remaining in this territory. Have you heard of him?" I asked.

"Yes, he is the *wkema*… leader… of a group that lives along the *Sakiwasipi* River. The French call it '*La Rivière des Miamis,*' the River of the Miamis, but the English know it as the 'Saint Joseph River.' Will you tell me why he is so important?" White Moon asked.

"My vision was more like a premonition – a feeling that something very bad could happen – was not clear. I think he is the key to your people staying in the Michigan Territory," I said in explanation.

"Marcus, it could take weeks to find him. I know his band occasionally travels along the Old Sauk Trail, but they are unpredictable," White Moon said, the panic rising in her voice. She sensed, as did I, that delaying our crossing of the time barrier as her pregnancy advanced brought with it numerous risks.

"Perhaps we could ask Running Deer to take She-Eagle and find Leopold Pokagon," I suggested. "Grandmother She-Eagle is widely respected."

"We must ask her," White Moon responded without even thinking, "but what is she to tell *wkema* Pokagon?"

"She will tell him that he has to figure out a way to make his followers become 'civilized'' or they will not be allowed to stay," I said.

"I understand," White Moon answered, "our band here has already given up some of their ways to follow the Cross, but our elders insisted that we keep as many of our other traditions as we can."

"Leopold Pokagon will know what to do," I said. "My vision tells me he will be successful."

*　*　*　*　*

She-Eagle was a wise woman and understood the importance of what we were telling her. It was nearly midnight when she called for Running Deer to come to her lodge.

"Running Deer," I said, "you need to take Grandmother She-Eagle west to the Saint Joseph River and find a man

324

called Leopold Pokagon. Once you find him, she will give him a message.”

Running Deer replied, “We will leave at dawn. I need to get my weapons ready –”

White Moon interrupted, “Brother, you know the legends of the travelers that come to us from other times. Marcus and I will become travelers tonight as well.”

“I was there when Miss Lizzie disappeared, sister. You must be careful,” he admonished.

“Marcus will not do to me what Stephen Wilcox did to Lizzie… we will not be going from the carved tree,” White Moon told her brother.

“There is another way?” Running Deer asked.

“Yes. Marcus explained it to me, and I understand it, but it uses numbers and pyramid shapes to give travelers a more exact destination in time. I wish I could explain it better,” said White Moon.

“I think the less I try to know, the better it is for me,” Running Deer teased.

Turning back to me, White Moon asked, “With Grandmother She-Eagle and Running Deer leaving in the morning, do you think we could leave tonight ourselves?”

"I think so…" I replied. "We certainly don't need to worry about finding Leopold Pokagon ourselves now. I suggest, though, that we rest for a couple of hours before stacking the musket balls."

"Marcus, I know I need my rest for the baby's sake, but I am too excited to sleep. Shouldn't we just stack the musket balls and see what happens?" said White Moon.

"We could but when we get to 2014, I will need you to be as alert as a hunter stalking a deer," I replied.

Throwing caution to the wind, we began stacking the musket balls in the small clearing to the north of our lodge. Because the entire Potawatomi village was aware of the legend of time travelers, there was no need to hide like we did when Stephen Wilcox made his jump several weeks earlier. Together, we laid the perimeter for the eight-by-eight base layer, ensuring that the prime apex was oriented to the north and that we were creating the perimeter in a clockwise direction, working through the east, south, and west compass points. I assumed that clockwise had enabled forward time travel and hoped that it had worked for Stephen Wilcox.

As we worked, I suddenly remembered the back-breaking effort that was required to stack the cannonballs on South Bass Island. Two hundred and four of them, each weighing approximately six pounds. *"Wait a minute,"* I thought to myself, *"was my memory of the future... my own real timeline... gradually returning to me?"*

When we began positioning the third layer of the pyramid, we both heard – but didn't feel – a low rumbling sound, like a laden freight train passing through a tunnel. It was truly a strange sound that should have been accompanied by vibrations. I knew we had heard it before and still had no logical explanation other than that it was connected with an upcoming jump across time. *Our* jump across time. The rumbling was one of the indicators that time travel was about to happen. The next thing would be the unexplained attraction between non-magnetic articles like the lead musket balls. The blue flash seemed to mark the opening and closing of the time portal – which we likely would not see ourselves.

Slowly and methodically, we began stacking the fourth layer. The rumbling increased in volume, and we finally began feeling subtle vibrations beneath our feet. That sensation increased through layers five and six and became almost uncomfortably and annoyingly loud as we stacked the four balls of level seven.

Locking my gaze on White Moon and she on mine, we somehow managed to grip the final musket ball, number 204, together in pincer grips between the thumbs and forefingers of our right hands. As we lifted the musket ball together to its intended place at the top of the pyramid, an unseen force took over and compelled us towards the apex.

The expression on White Moon's face was one of wonder and amazement. She seemed to sense that something was changing as the final musket ball was less than an inch from its resting place. We could no longer resist the pull of the pyramid even if we wanted to, and the ball clicked solidly in place. With a blink of an eye, everything changed.

37: 2018

Before we could even blink, woodland sounds were replaced by those of industry and mechanization. All familiar to me, but they were frightening to White Moon... Luna... and she covered her ears to block them out.

"Marcus, what are these terrible noises I am hearing?" she pleaded.

"You are hearing the sounds of my time, your future, my dear," I said with a smile just as a police siren began blaring.

"It sounds like a death wail. Make it stop, please!" she pleaded. Her tone was frantic and ululating.

"I can't," I said matter-of-factly.

"The noise is making our baby jump around inside me," she said.

That was one of the things I wanted desperately to hear from my wife: that our baby seemed to be okay and had made it through the time portal. I was truly relieved, as I knew that one of the indicators of fetal distress was a lack of movement. Luna had just confirmed that all was presumably well. I tried not to let my emotions distract me, though, as I needed my wits about me in case things suddenly took a dangerous turn.

Checking our surroundings, I knew we were in a park of some kind, and it seemed vaguely familiar. Taking Luna by the hand, I led her towards a clearing so that I could take stock of our situation and perhaps figure out where we were; within a few steps, we were on an asphalt-paved footpath and heading into the clearing.

My military training took over and I instinctively scanned the clearing and its perimeter for threats. There was no one else within visual range, so I assumed it was safe for us to proceed across the open space towards a sign that I hoped would provide information on our whereabouts.

The sign was full of useful tidbits. Across the top, the words "Palmer Park" were emblazoned in brilliant green letters. Below the words was a rudimentary map of the trails going to the left and right. To the right was Witherell Woods; to the left, picnic pavilions, a parking lot, and rest rooms.

"Palmer Park!" I exclaimed quite loudly, frightening Luna almost as much as the police siren a few minutes earlier. "I know this place. We would come here when we were skipping class at the Catholic High School for boys just down the road to the west."

Luna's expression told me she didn't understand what I was trying to explain.

"In this time, everyone is supposed to go to school until they are approximately 18 years old," I explained, "and it was expected that even the 'good kids' would skip… miss… class every once in a while."

"How did they hunt? How did they plant and harvest if all the children were attending school?" Luna asked.

"That's one of the many things I will have to teach you about this time," I answered. "Children start going to school when they are about 5 years old."

"I would like to hear more about school, Marcus. Will our child have to go to school as well?" she asked.

"Yes," I answered. "We could home-school our children if we wish, but I think we have to get approval from the authorities before we can do that. It can be a confusing process."

"I have so much to learn," Luna said as she began to cry.

"The first thing we need to be worried about is food and a place to stay. We also need some clothing that is more appropriate to this time. We look like we just stepped out of a Jane Austen novel," I said somewhat sarcastically, waving my hands at my own sartorial splendor.

"Who is Jane Austen?"

"She is a famous British writer from your time," I explained.

For some unexplained reason, we were drawn towards the Witherell Woods path and not the other direction towards the pavilions and restrooms. Something was forcing us away from civilization and deeper into the woods. We didn't have to wait for very long to find out why.

Luna saw it first: the circle carving in a tree. It appeared to have been freshly carved but was identical to the one in the tree near her home village from 1814. If it was indeed the same carving, I was curious about how it managed to remain fresh and unweathered.

"Marcus, this is the same place where Stephen Wilcox sent Lizzie across time," said Luna.

"Yes, I believe it is, but look how the carving still looks as if it were just done yesterday," I pointed out. "Maybe we just need to accept that the carving will always remain fresh and possessed by some mystical force or being. That would be true to the traditions of your people, my darling."

"What drew us here? We should have gone the other direction from the sign, towards civilization, and not deeper into the forest," Luna commented.

"I don't know, but I think we are being sent a message that if we ever want to make a jump in time, this carving will always be here for us."

*　*　*　*　*

We prepared to spend our first night in 2018 in a remote area of Palmer Park that was not likely to be patrolled by the Detroit Police Department. Thanks to our combined survival skills, we were able to stay warm and dry without building a fire that certainly would have drawn someone's attention, attention that we did not need.

As we readied for sleep, I patted myself down and realized that my wallet, which had disappeared when I jumped to 1814, was now back in my pocket along with my military retiree ID, driver's license and credit cards. Checking another pocket, I discovered my cell phone was there. I turned it on and, surprisingly, it was almost fully charged. I could not control my elation.

"Luna! Look! It's all of my things that I thought had disappeared when I went to 1814. Everything that proves I am me is right here. I can use these cards for money so we can eat. I can buy appropriate clothing. We can also rent a car and drive to my home in Virginia," I explained. She was most curious about the cell phone when I placed a call to the rental car agency.

The look on her face told me that she had no idea what I was talking about. Military IDs, credit cards, driver's licenses, and cars did not exist in her time, nor did even the most rudimentary telephone. I had some serious explaining to do, a process that I imagined would take days, if not weeks or months, to complete.

There was also the matter of Luna's existence. How were we going to make her a real person in the eyes of the law? Assuming she had been born in the United States, she would already have had things like a Birth Certificate, Social Security Number, and maybe a passport or "green card" to document her existence. It was going to be a challenge to get it all sorted out before our child was born and the time came for us to provide information for the baby's Birth Certificate.

We found temporary lodging at a motel near the park, It was not much more than a flop house, but better than sleeping rough in the park – something that the Detroit authorities frowned upon. I had to get Luna up to speed on modern conveniences and lifestyle quickly and the lack of distractions at the motel would simplify my task.

Luna, it turned out, was a fast learner and able to assimilate and retain information better than any ring-knockers – those Naval Academy graduates who draw attention to their self-important status by knocking their inverted rings against a table in meetings – I had met in all of my assignments. I wondered if Luna might even have an untested eidetic memory.

Within a week, she was ready for our first foray in an automobile, a convertible that I had acquired on a one-way rental contract from Detroit's Metropolitan Airport to Newport News/Williamsburg International Airport in Virginia. It was nominally a 10-hour drive, but with Luna's advancing pregnancy and almost perpetual need to use the restroom, I envisioned a total of more like 13 or 14 hours.

Luna was amazed by the speed at which we traveled and at first became a little bit nauseated from the unfamiliar motion. I helped her overcome that sensation by putting the top down and flooding the car with fresh air. She relished the moment with childlike enthusiasm. "It's like riding a horse into a thunderstorm!" she squealed with delight.

At one of our frequent stops, Luna asked me, "Marcus, when you were in my time, did you miss all of this?"

"Why would I miss it if I had you back then? I didn't have a choice about being there, but I certainly made the best of it," I teased. She and our growing child were truly the only things that mattered in the past, present, or future and I wanted to be sure she knew it.

By the time we reached Richmond on Interstate 95, Luna had fully accepted and embraced the 21st Century. She quickly decided she liked fast food, frou-frou coffee, and high-speed car travel with the top down – understanding that we would be making a trip in less than a day that would have taken people from 1814 up to two weeks to complete.

We reached Newport News, turned in the rental car, and took a taxi from there to my home on Langley Air Force Base, which had recently converted some of its housing to rental accommodations available to retired military personnel. We were home.

Next on my list was establishing Luna's legal personhood. I knew a forger, a refugee from one of my can't-talk-about-it assignments, who could easily provide us with the necessary documents like a Birth Certificate and Marriage Certificate to get the process started. I was certain that the forger, whose status as a refugee was the result of my sponsorship, would help. He lived in a trailer park not far from the base.

I decided it would be ill-advised for Luna to go with me to visit the forger. We didn't need to cloud her existence by allowing her association with nefarious activity, albeit indirectly. It would be the first time for me to leave her alone in the 21st century.

"Luna, will you be okay staying here and watching television or reading a book?" I asked. "I have some business to take care of, and it would not be appropriate for you to be there with me."

"Yes, Marcus. I find what you call 'westerns' very funny. They always make the Natives seem like they are such savages," she giggled.

"I will be back in a couple of hours," I told her.

*　*　*　*　*

"What is the child's name?" the hospital clerk asked us. "We need to apply for a Virginia Certificate of Live Birth.

Luna answered before I could even open my mouth. "Sean Marcus Harris." She had chosen those names to honor both her father and me.

"Could you spell those names for me, please?" the clerk asked. "It might be easier if you wrote them down on this paper; I will transfer that to the computer."

I obliged, printing in block capitals our son's name. Had she not asked for confirmation in writing, I probably would have answered in NATO phonetics. I was giddy with elation and the entire situation was surreal.

"Sir, I have a few more questions to ask, if I may… Mrs. Harris, where were you born?"

Luna looked at me; she seemed perplexed by how to answer the question. Our son chose that very moment to begin wailing with hunger, which gave me the opportunity I needed to answer on Luna's behalf as Luna slowly uncovered herself to allow our son to nurse.

"Michigan. Detroit, Michigan," was my succinct reply.

"Do you know her date of birth, Mr. Harris?" The clerk's condescending tone told me she had noticed the difference in our ages.

"March 9, 1995," I answered.

"And your date of birth, sir?" Again, the condescending tone was making me angry.

"June 29, 1974," I snapped.

"So Mrs. Harris is 23 and you are 44… hmm…"

It was like I was sitting with the 'church lady' of a popular late-night comedy routine. I was almost ready to demand that the woman leave Luna's room immediately.

"Marcus," Luna interrupted, sensing my growing frustration with the situation, "could you get me some ice chips, please?"

"Yes, my dear," I answered, taking a deep breath and reaching for the ice bucket on her bedside table. The distraction calmed me down, but only slightly.

"Mr. Harris, what is your current occupation?" the clerk asked.

"I am a retired Naval Special Warfare Operator," I answered. Subconsciously, I think I wanted her to know that I was a trained killer. I could have simply answered "retired Navy," but I could not resist the temptation of the veiled threat.

"And Lena?" she asked, raising a single disdainful eyebrow. I found her use of the wrong first name to be disrespectful.

"That's 'Mrs. Harris' to you… and her name is Luna, not Lena. She is a homemaker and will be taking care of our son," I said.

Turning back to Luna, the clerk made one of those faces, with her single eyebrow raised and her lips pursed as she asked the next question: "Mrs. Harris, is Sean Marcus the natural child of you… and your… husband?"

At that point, I had had enough and stopped Luna from answering.

"Ma'am, I would appreciate it very much if you left your personal biases outside of this room." I said in a tone that was all business.

With as much sarcasm as I could muster, I continued, "If you must know, Mrs. Harris was abducted by intergalactic travelers in 1814 and impregnated with an alien phallus while on their spaceship. They dropped her off here in 2018. I fed her and she came home with me, just like a little puppy dog. She hasn't left my side since then."

"Mr. Harris, this conversation is over," the clerk said with a huff, "and I will be back tomorrow with the Birth Certificate. Good evening." The clerk, whose name I never did catch, stood up and stormed out of the room, her chunky heels clacking double-time on the tiled floor of the maternity hall.

Before the clerk was even out of earshot, both Luna and I erupted in raucous laughter. We were loud enough that the charge nurse came bustling from the nurses' station to insist that we lower our voices. We quickly complied, knowing that my remaining in the room overnight was a privilege, not a right, and that I could be asked to leave at any time.

With Sean settling down for another sleep, I eased myself onto the hospital bed next to Luna. Within minutes, she was asleep in my arms. As I lay there next to her, listening to both her and our son breathe softly, tears of happiness welled up in my eyes. Never could I have imagined the twists and turns my life had taken since that fateful day on South Bass Island, and I wouldn't trade it for anything else.

Author Notes

The foundation for this book are a couple of very vague military records that suggest a Curtis J. Hurd, postulated to be my fourth great-granduncle, was a Surgeon's Mate in the War of 1812, serving in a Connecticut militia regiment. That person is represented by the character of Doctor Stephen Wilcox in this book. Other connections to a familial westward migration from New London, Connecticut, following the burning of the town by Benedict Arnold are covered in Book Two of the Lineage Series, "Soldier, Citizen, Settler."

The War of 1812 is probably the most poorly documented of any of the United States' military conflicts. Specific battles like the naval Battle of Lake Erie, the Battle of Baltimore, and the sacking of Washington, DC, however, are well-documented. Even so, I took considerable literary license with modes of transportation, military weaponry, and communications (or lack thereof) to craft the stories of the main characters.

The Battle of Lake Erie gave us Commodore Oliver Hazard Perry and his famous "We have met the enemy and he is ours" dispatch to future President, General William

Henry Harrison. The Battle of Baltimore gave us "The Star Spangled Banner," and the sacking of Washington, DC, saw the White House burned and the U.S. Capitol occupied by a foreign enemy force before it, too, was burned.

Fort Malden, in the present-day Amherstburg, Ontario, is a real place. It was abandoned and destroyed by the British shortly after their defeat on Lake Erie. The new occupants, the American army, attempted to restore some of its fortifications, but abandoned those efforts after the Treaty of Ghent was signed in late 1814, before the fort was returned to British control in 1815.

The War of 1812 was heavily influenced by Native American participation. A loose confederation of Native nations sided with the British and fought under Tecumseh before he was killed at the so-called Battle of the Thames, mentioned in Chapter 12. The Americans, on the other hand, enjoyed very little Native support.

The Potawatomi band that gave us the characters of She-Eagle, White Moon, Running Deer, and Chipmunk is fictitious. However, Leopold Pokagon was a real leader; a modern band of Potawatomi is named after him, having its tribal seat in Dowagiac, Berrien County, Michigan. Unlike the rest of the Potawatomi who were "removed" to western reservations under President Andrew Jackson, Leopold Pokagon found a loophole that allowed him and his followers to remain in Michigan as modernized Christian tribesmen.

The possibilities of time travel or life in planetary systems have always fascinated me. It was time travel that gave me a creative way of bringing history alive in this book and its predecessor, "Of Time and Place.". To some, history is boring – but not to me. I choose to embrace our history and firmly believe in Winston Churchill's admonition, "those that fail to learn from history are doomed to repeat it."

Acknowledgments

As always, I could not have written this book without the support and encouragement of my wife, Sandy. We will celebrate 44 years of marriage in June, not long after this book will have been released.

A former work colleague, mentor, Jeopardy contestant, and sometimes YouTube interviewer, Diane Mezzanotte inspired me to try my hand at time-hopping and dual timeline narrative. I have found this format exhilarating and refreshing, always keeping me on my toes. Thanks, Diane!

I also have to thank my friends, David Wilson and Freddy Krieger, for their interest in my work. Dave, as a retired detective, has been invaluable with his input to several of my books. Freddy, a retired Lutheran pastor and amateur historian, shares a common interest in genealogy and research. He, too, has provided honest feedback on this and previous works.

I also have to acknowledge the other authors on the Lineage Independent Publishing team who have kept me motivated (and in some cases, re-motivated me) to keep going to the end, especially Patricia Donoghue (aka G.B. Carmichael), Rebecca Conaty Bruce, and Lisa Talbott.

While dealing with life events of their own, they still managed to provide much-needed words of encouragement when I needed them most.

I am eternally grateful to Lorna Hart for her artistic talent and creativity. With minimal guidance she has provided the artwork for the back cover and internal graphics.

Finally, to Martin Radford (aka Beck Hilliard), I have to acknowledge that it was your insistence that made me consider audiobooks as a viable outlet for our works. When Amazon came calling with an offer for us to participate in their beta release of a new "virtual voice narration" capability, I was ready and willing. As a result, most of the Lineage library is now available in audiobook format.

Michael Paul Hurd

Author / Publisher

Lineage Independent Publishing